LATE
for the
FUNERAL

LATE
for the
FUNERAL

Douglas and Dorothy
STAPLETON

COACHWHIP PUBLICATIONS
Greenville, Ohio

Late for the Funeral, by Douglas and Dorothy Stapleton
© 2023 Coachwhip Publications edition
Front cover: 1950 Flxible Funeral Coach commercial ad,
    via Alden Jewell

First published 1953
Douglas Stapleton, 1907-1972
Dorothy Stapleton, 1917-1970
CoachwhipBooks.com

ISBN 1-61646-543-3
ISBN-13 978-1-61646-543-8

CHAPTER 1

"You'll be late for your funeral!"

Bill Taylor flung it back through the still half-open door, trying to keep it light, making a teasing phrase for Penny's light-hearted and habitual lateness. Only this time it had gotten under his skin because Penny knew only too well how important this appointment was. Good Lord, she had even taken the phone call! Angry with himself for letting Penny make him angry, he slammed the door.

He looked at the solidity of the door as if he could still see it vibrating. A month ago I'd never have done that, he told himself, and jammed his hat on the back of his head.

At the curb, his hand on the door of the car, he glanced back, half expecting Penny to fling open the house door and call out to him to wait, she'd be ready in a minute. If he did, he'd wait, even though he knew it would be many minutes, and he had that appointment with Bedford. He glanced down at the thin platinum wrist watch imbedded in the dark hairs of his wrist. Looking at it, he grinned. Me with a platinum wrist watch—pink ribbons on a baboon. The watch had been Uncle Ralph's wedding present to him, probably a not too subtle reminder that even a construction engineer doesn't have to be an oaf. But I am an oaf. He could see, reflected in the curved watch crystal, a miniature of his face. It was the face of an oaf.

Square jaw and big mouth, a flat nose made even flatter
in the Rose Bowl game five years back, above it thick black
streaks of eyebrows that almost met, and under the now
straightened hat a brush of hair with all the glimmer and
softness of an old curry comb. He waggled his finger at
the reflection. That's me, Bill Taylor, oaf. You're a throwback. Fine old families that produce thoroughbreds like
Uncle Ralph shouldn't have to contend with a Mick Irish
throwback.

Bill grinned, and the reflection offered a miniature
grin that crinkled all the way up to the eyes. Somewhere
back in the sedate old family of Taylors there must have
been a quiet scandal, and he was the late and living proof.
He chuckled and then looked beyond the reflection at the
dial of the watch itself. He'd stood there nearly two minutes—time enough for Penny to get over her mad and call
him, if she was ever going to. He glanced back at the front
door surreptitiously and then found his eyes dragged to
an upstairs window. Penny stood there, her bright gold
hair catching the sunlight, her oval, elfin face tilted down
and sidewise, peering at him, her arms folded across her
breasts as if she were hugging her anger to her. She must
have seen him glance up, because she stepped back from
the window, leaving it blank and naked, like the space of
a suddenly yanked tooth.

Bill flung himself in the car and tramped on the starter,
hard, barely letting the engine catch before he wheeled the
car into traffic. Now whatever made an unimaginative guy
like me think of a thing like that—the space of a suddenly
yanked tooth? He knew the answer: because seeing her leave
the window so suddenly had hurt. But why had it hurt?
Then he knew why. Penny was dressed, ready to go, and she
hadn't come down to ride with him. That was what they had
argued about—that Penny was never dressed in the morning
in time to go with him when she was going to need the car,

or wanted a lift to go shopping. And this morning, when he so desperately needed time, she had come to breakfast wrapped to her lovely throat in a scarlet dressing gown, or hostess gown, or whatever women called those overelaborate excuses for not getting dressed in the morning.

He swung the car away from town, feeling the warmth of late spring in the air without realizing it, and it softened his scowl into a smile. Penny had been teasing him. Under that elaborate gown she'd been dressed and ready to go, waiting until the last minute to throw it off and show him she was really ready for once. And that was the morning he had to go and lose his temper! Bill Taylor, you *are* an oaf, and you've got to make it up to Penny.

And there was such a lot to make up for. The idea of a girl like Penny, a girl who had everything—looks, figure, family and a career—giving it all up to marry an oaf like Bill Taylor, and a poor oaf at that. First, as soon as this deal was closed, he'd give Penny a car of her own. Oh, maybe not as fancy as that Caddy convertible she'd been driving when he met her four months ago at Uncle Ralph's, but something pretty good. Maybe a Buick. Convertible, with dark green leather upholstery to show off Penny's gilt-blonde hair. And then, when he'd finished this contract, he'd build her a house, a very modern house. Penny would love that. She was a perfect kid about shiny bright gadgets and sleek, modern furniture.

Daydreaming, he almost overshot the side road. He backed, turned and bumped down it, mentally calculating the cubic yards of bed-gravel, aggregate and cement needed to make this a fitting entrance to the new subdivision. The grading wasn't bad. Two bulldozers could level it for surfacing. Drainage looks good. Might dam that creek and make a private lake. Spot the houses along the knolls.

He pulled up beside a farmhouse that had once been uncompromisingly foursquare and now sagged drunkenly on the hilltop, not even worth dismantling for timber and certainly not quaint enough to be worth restoring. Mentally Bill yanked it down and substituted a rambling, ranch-type club house with a wide overhang and several terraces as the center and heart of the new subdivision. A tarmac parking area there, the pool there. Behind those poplars he'd put tennis courts. And through there . . . Bill was happily lost in the combination of dreaming and mathematics that was his career. Bedford Acres would be a place for gracious living. And some day he and Penny would live there.

He was pacing off a road frontage when the sun winked on the wrist watch swinging with his stride. He held it up, stared at it unbelievingly. Eleven-thirty! Dick, his partner, Dick Barnes, and Old Man Bedford should have been here over an hour ago. Had he missed hearing them? He loped back up the hill to the leaning farmhouse and peered around. Could they have come and, not seeing him, gone again? Dick wouldn't have done that, not with Bill's old Chevvy in plain sight. No, something had held them up. Maybe Old Man Bedford, like Penny, was a slow starter. Or, and Bill had a quick flash of hope, maybe the old man was already signing a Barnes & Taylor contract without bothering to go over the grounds. Bill sank down on the broken steps of the farmhouse. That last was not likely, not with a shrewd old duck like Anthony Bedford.

An hour later Bill scowled at his wrist watch as if it had betrayed him. Some hitch must have developed. Or Old Man Bedford could have called the whole thing off. He had to fight a moment of panic. But if Bedford had called off the deal, Dick would have driven out to tell him. Or he'd have sent Janet, their secretary-receptionist-typist and general office manager.

Still feeling a little uncertain, Bill turned the car around and bumped back over the clay-gravel road, turning back toward town and a service station he had spotted. His nickel bonged in the phone box and a detached voice informed him it was a toll call, deposit fifteen cents, please. He had to ask the surly attendant for change for a dollar before he could make the call. He didn't have the exact change but he handed Bill a dime, took the dollar. Bill dropped the dime in, heard the double ping and got through to Janet.

"Hey, Janet, what the devil happened to Dick?"

"Bill!" Janet's warm, breathy voice caught in a little hiccough, became flat, very flat and impersonal. "I'll let you talk to Mister Barnes. . . ."

He started to ask her why the formality and then hoped that Old Man Bedford was there. There! Right then! And the deal was still on. He grinned at the phone, worries dissipated. He heard the rattle of Dick's receiver and Dick's deep, resonant salesman's voice. "Bill!" That sudden warmth, and then controlled calmness. "Bill, I think you'd better go home. Right away. I'll meet you there."

The black cylinder of the phone receiver skidded in the sudden cold sweat of Bill's hand. His voice, when he tried to speak, caught in his throat like a physical thing. He coughed it up. "Penny! Something's happened to Penny!" Distantly, almost unaware of it, he heard a sob and then the rattling click of Janet's extension being hung up. "Is it bad, Dick?"

"I don't know, Bill. They didn't tell me. But they're trying to locate you. Go on home. I'll meet you there." He hesitated a moment and then added, "And don't worry." The phone clicked into humming futility.

Bill stared down the receiver as if through it he could see the office, see Dick's calm, careful face, Janet's puckish grin, and read them. Looking at the phone reminded him he could call the house. And Penny would answer and assure him everything was all right, that she'd just got panicky about a man skulking in the back yard and called the police. Penny was always thinking she saw men skulking in back yards.

He whirled on the attendant. "Gimme my change!" and snatched it from the outstretched hand, barely noticing the darkening scowl and only half hearing the boy say, "Sure you don't want your shoes shined, too?"

The instant he'd snatched the change Bill was ashamed, but his big hand had turned to numb, non-functioning sausage fingers that could sort out the coins, and he couldn't stop to apologize. Finally he separated a nickel and a dime and dropped them in the slots and then couldn't remember his own phone number. After several false starts he got it right and waited, hearing the burr-burr—pause—burr-burr.

Now Penny would hear it and turn away from the policeman, telling him, over one slim shoulder, that she was sorry to have bothered him and would he excuse her while she answered the phone. Now she'd be running down the hall, dodging the console that was just a little too big. Now she's reaching for the phone. Now . . .

The burr-burr stopped abruptly.

A man's hoarse, metallic voice said, "Hello!" And then: "There's a guy on the phone, Loot."

The phone changed hands. Bill could hear the sharp click of a man's heavy ring hitting the mouthpiece and a distant voice was saying, "I'll take it, Casey." And then a crisp, pleasant, "Hello. Who's speaking?"

It was so mildly casual Bill felt instant relief. So much so that he stammered. "B-Bill Taylor. M-may I speak to Penny? My wife, Mrs. Taylor."

"I don't think she can come to the phone right this minute, Taylor. Could you come on home? There's been a little trouble. . . ."

So Penny was there but couldn't come to the phone. She was probably out in the kitchen, serving drinks and laughing with the men from the radio squad car, or more likely out in the yard, pointing out just where she'd seen the skulking figure. And there'd be at least six policemen with her. Penny always managed to have men around her.

"I'll be right home. And tell Penny not to worry. I'll be right home," he repeated senselessly.

"Sure, Taylor. I'll tell her. And come right on home. By the way where are you?"

"Service station, out by the Bedford place. See you in fifteen minutes."

"Do that." The voice was so casually amiable that Bill felt like chortling. Imagine, getting the wind up, just because Dick got stuffy on the phono. He hung up, so relieved he slapped the rest of the change into the surly attendant's hand, and ran for the car.

At home, he vaulted the front steps, paused, cautioning himself. It was only a burglary. He reached for the knob and felt it slide out of his hand. A slim, compact man in blue cheviot pulled the door inward and nodded to Bill. It took a second's adjustment before he realized the man wasn't small. It was just that Bill himself was so big.

"I'm Charlie Fentress." The man jerked his head toward the phone Bill could see over his shoulder. "The 'loot.'" He smiled and held out his hand.

"I'm Bill Taylor."

"I know." The hand tugged Bill inside and guided him into his own living room.

Odd, being ushered into your own living room, as if you were a visitor. You saw it with new eyes and realized the damask drapes were too metallically blue. And the rug looked garish, a plaintive attempt at dusty rose that somehow wound up cerise. Maybe it only looked shoddy because he was coming into the room by daylight instead of at night, as he usually did, to find Penny shining and brushed and glamorous in it. Or maybe it only needed Penny's vividness to tone all this slightly off-beat and meretricious stuff into gay and dramatic harmony. Now those white plaster wall brackets were good—a little cold and stark, maybe, for a house that wasn't meant to be modern. But they were good. Dick's wedding gift. And there was a heavy brass candlestick Uncle Ralph had given . . . No. That was missing. Penny must have put it away. She'd never really liked it. Bill swung around, tangling his big feet in the white shag rug. Fentress steadied him, pushed him backward into a deep, soft chair.

"Let's sit down and talk this over."

Bill hadn't intended to sit and he didn't want to talk anything over. He wanted to see Penny, hear her voice, touch the brightness of her hair. But he sat. Charlie Fentress was more of a man than you'd think under that trim blue suit.

"It wasn't burglary." Bill said it without inflection, without hope, and then looked up quickly, hoping that Fentress would give him a last-minute reprieve. He didn't.

"No. It wasn't burglary."

"I've been hoping . . ."

"I know. We always hope. . . ."

"Why didn't you tell me, when I phoned?"

"It was better to hope, wasn't it?"

Bill closed his eyes hotly, fought one last, staggering round against realization, and lost. That phrase "wasn't it" set the seal on it. Past tense. Finished. Done. No more hope. He brought his voice up over the anguish in his throat.

"She's dead?" It was one last, futile question.

"Yes."

It must be true but it seemed impossible to get it through his head. He had to say it aloud.

"Penny is dead."

He looked up at Fentress, not seeing him, just a fuzzy outline that was human, that could listen and nod and maybe speak words.

"It's a silly thing to remember, maybe sillier to have said. But just this morning I told Penny she'd be late to her own funeral. She's always late, you know. . . . But this time she's early, early to her own funeral . . . years early . . . so many years early!"

And Bill Taylor was crying.

Chapter II

Bill yanked violently at his handkerchief and blew his nose, trying to smile at Fentress. "Sorry, Lieutenant. I'm too big to cry."

Fentress leaned on the mantel, his back to Bill. "You're big all right, Taylor, but you're never too big to cry." His voice cracked and died. His finger slid along the mantel, caught a framed photograph of Penny and turned it hastily away. "She was a darned beautiful woman."

Bill found himself thinking abstractedly that it wasn't a good picture of Penny, not as he remembered her. Too glamorized, too calculatedly voluptuous to be the gay, vivid woman he had known. The picture lied about Penny, but he could see where another man might find it, and the woman it portrayed, beautiful. Only, somehow, he hadn't expected it of Fentress.

"You're a funny cop." As soon as he said it he realized that that, too, was odd. Perhaps I'm the one who's seen too many movies.

"I'm not a cop, Taylor." Fentress swung around, hunching his shoulder against the mantel. "I'm an attorney and investigator for the district attorney's office. I'm not even really a lieutenant." He grinned. "It just eases Casey's official conscience to give me the rank. He'd hate taking orders from a civilian."

"I had a sergeant like that. Rank-conscious. Only he hated lieutenants."

"Nothing less than a captain for him, huh? I notice my rank fluctuates with the crew I'm working with. This one is headed by a sergeant, a very smart sergeant, so I'm a lieutenant. For today."

"Subject to change without notice? Must be bewildering."

Fentress spread his hands, grinning. "I've learned to adjust. I know Casey's talking to me when he uses a tone that suggests a cross between dog-trainer and mother of a slightly backward child. A basso mother."

"I know that tone. I was the backward child. Too big and awkward. I grew up in terror of small tables and large vases. Clumsy as anything."

"Till they gave you a football."

"You know about that?"

"Saw you in the Rose Bowl game."

Bill fingered the battered hump on his pose, remembering. So it came as a surprise when Fentress straightened and came over to stand by his chair. "Think you can stand it now? Identifying her?"

Bill heaved himself up, momentarily furious with Fentress for trying to coddle him. The other man must have sensed it. "We need you, Bill, to help us catch the man who did it."

His whole big frame shook with that. Murder! It couldn't be murder! He was halfway upstairs before Fentress' voice caught him.

"Where the devil are you going?"

"To Penny." And he kept on.

"She's down here. In the kitchen." Fentress pointed.

Bill had to stoop to peer through the banisters at Fentress. He came back dazedly, wondering why he had dashed upstairs. I know. Because that's the last place I saw her.

She was standing at the window, looking at me. And because Penny just hadn't seemed made for kitchens, and certainly not to die in one.

"Why didn't you tell me?" He swung around the newel post and brushed past Fentress. "We've been wasting time."

"Not much." Fentress caught at his arm. "Wait! It's messy."

The warning came too late. Bill had already thrust open the swinging door and seen her.

The next few minutes were a blur of pictures that stopped and ran at dizzying speeds and stopped again, like a film projector gone crazy. The kitchen, full of the blue backs of policemen that parted like a curtain so that he could see Penny crumpled there. Her scarlet housecoat, the outflung hand with scarlet fingernails and the tiny wink of diamonds in her combination wedding-and-engagement ring. I was going to get her a big diamond when I got rich. And Penny's head face down, pressed hard against the floor, her gilt-gold hair streaming out in that sticky red mess on the floor, as if the scarlet housecoat had got wet and run. And Uncle Ralph's big brass candlestick at his feet. He almost stumbled over it. He could remember his own voice saying, "Turn her over. Turn her over. Turn her over." Like a cracked record. And Fentress saying, "Better not." Only somebody reached out and turned her over, soggily, squashily, so that dead, lack-lustre eyes stared up at him out of a battered and bloody face.

And there the picture stuck. And then went blurrily crazy. Memory stuck there, too, and didn't come back until he felt two men holding him in the big chair in the living room and looked up to see Fentress moving his jaw gingerly and shrugging his coat into shape.

Bill lurched against the restraining hands. "I'll kill the murdering—"

"You don't have to practice on my policemen."

Bill looked up at the two men holding him. He nodded and sank back, watching them withdraw their hands slowly. He thrust out his tongue to wet his lips and realized one of them was puffy. "Is an apology any good?"

"I think the boys understand."

Both policemen nodded, and one of them gave Bill a smile of grudging admiration. "You sure work fast, mister. I never even got my stick out." He grinned wider. "And the doc is still working on Casey."

Bill almost didn't hear that. He was clutching wildly at some picture of Penny as she had been, even a clear one of her angry with him, glaring from an upstairs window. Anything would do, if it would clear his mind of that other picture of Penny that wasn't Penny any more. What was that the cop had said? Oh, yes. He looked at Fentress.

"Is Casey hurt?"

"Out colder'n a mackerel," one of the cops answered for him.

"I'm sorry." Bill shivered. "When they tried to keep me from her . . ."

Fentress nodded. "It's understandable, Taylor."

"But did you have to do it like that?" Bill shivered again.

"Routine." The harsh, deep voice came from behind, and Bill jerked his head around. A stocky man stood spraddle-legged in the archway to the hall, rubbing the back of his neck with a wet dish towel, so that his head bent downward and sidewise. "Do it like that with all suspects. Shock treatment." He pulled the towel over his balding spot till it hooded him, like a prize fighter leaving the ring, and rolled his head stiffly on a red, leathery neck. "Routine." The stocky man locked his fingers behind his neck and rocked his head against them. "You pack a mean wallop."

All in a deep, harsh monotone. Even the last statement held no animosity. A statement of fact.

Finally the stocky man's words penetrated. "Suspect?" Bill swung his eyes to Fentress. "You think I could have . . ."

"Routine," the stocky man answered. "Wife killed. Husband did it, nine times out of ten." He thought that over behind brooding, emotionless eyes and then upped the odds. "Ninety-nine times out of a hundred." The emotionless eyes turned to Fentress. "Want I should take him in, Loot?"

"Why, you . . ." Bill hurled himself out of the chair. The two cops broke his lunge, pinned him back where he lay, glaring up at Fentress. The investigator had winced, but the stocky man had stood stolidly watching. Now he nodded, as if the lunge had proved something.

Bill glared up at Fentress. "Are you going to let this man accuse me . . ."

Fentress pinched his lips flat. "Casey didn't accuse you, Taylor. He stated a fact. His figures may be a little off, but not much. I believe statistics show eighty-seven out of a hundred murders are family affairs. Husband kills wife. Wife kills husband. We look for the survivor—first."

Bill shook his head dully. "Then all that Big Brother Stuff was an act? A build-up for this?"

Fentress sighed and sat down opposite him. "Not all of it." A smile glimmered and was suppressed. "In fact, the part that was an act didn't go over so big. You ran in the wrong direction, among other things. That's why I can talk to you like this." He linked hands around one knee, pulling his foot off the floor, rocking slowly. "Our job is to catch the killer. If that's you, make no mistake, we'll catch you. But neither Casey"—he nodded toward the stocky man—"nor I, nor Pilsudski, nor O'Hara," he included the two cops by Bill's chair, "nor any man on the force will accuse you of anything. Not till we can prove it. It's standard procedure to take a man in, in a case like this. Establish motives, alibis, opportunity, stuff like that. Not only yours but those of anybody you know."

Bill shook his head violently. "Nobody would want to kill Penny."

"Somebody did."

Bill shuddered. "Yes, somebody did." He glanced at Fentress. "A maniac? One of those . . ."

"The doctor says not," said Fentress. "And the other evidence doesn't stack up that way."

"Evidence?" Even while his stomach churned and his throat was filled with stale cotton candy, he could ask questions. "How could you have evidence so quick?"

"Routine," Casey croaked from the archway.

"That's about it, Taylor. Routine. Not so much what's there as what's missing. Things we normally find in an attack case."

"Like what?" It had to be a maniac. Nobody wanted to kill Penny.

Fentress sighed. "Not enough struggle, for one thing. For another, she had a Scotch highball with the killer."

"Not Penny. She didn't like Scotch and she never drank before six." He said it triumphantly, as if that would prove that Penny wasn't dead.

"She did today. The glass had her fingerprints."

"Last night's drinks," he suggested, then rubbed his hand across his forehead. "No, we were at Dick's last night. My partner's place. But you wouldn't know that."

"We did, though. Routine again. We checked your office, looking for you, and Barnes told us. Anyway, the dregs are too fresh and there's a bit of ice left. In both drinks."

"Fingerprints!" Bill felt a surge of triumph. "His glass will have his fingerprints on it!"

Fentress killed his moment of triumph. "Wiped clean. And smashed. Oh, we've sent the pieces to the lab, but I doubt they'll find anything we didn't. And in our book maniacs or sluggers don't bother to wipe off fingerprints." Fentress checked his points with crisp nods. "No struggle. Friendly drink. No evidence of assault. No fingerprints. So it doesn't look like a maniac or tramp or skulker. We could be wrong. But we can change our minds." Fentress unclasped his hands and shook one finger at Bill. "That's our greatest advantage. We can change our minds. The killer can't. We can be wrong a hundred times, a thousand times. But if the killer is wrong just once"—Fentress pincered his hands together slowly—"we've got him. First one little discrepancy, then another, and then we've got him." His hands ground together as if crushing something repulsive.

"And I'll help you get him!" It was a pledge much deeper than the words, more than he meant Fentress to know. *If I find him, the police won't need to get him.*

"Okay." Fentress sat up suddenly, and it was almost as if he had rubbed his hands in anticipation of action. "Maybe now you can see the importance of negative clues, of things we can clear away, at least for the moment. You said you were at the Bedford farm. How long?"

There were noises out in the kitchen. Some men picking up a large and unwieldy bundle and carrying it out. "How long? Nine to nearly one."

"Over three hours? On a deserted farm?"

"We were planning a subdivision there."

"Anybody with you?"

Bill shook his head, scowling. "No. They didn't show up. Dick was to bring Old Man Bedford out this morning, but I guess this . . ." He waved jerkily toward the back of the house, where the gruesome noises were receding.

"How's that?"

Bill swiveled in his chair and saw Dick, trim and dapper and correct, in the archway. He started up, and Dick hurried forward. "Keep your seat, Bill," Dick's smoothly tanned hand pressed into Bill's shoulder as the older man turned to face Fentress. He nodded to Fentress with a courtesy as smooth as the attorney's.

"I'm Dick Barnes, Bill's partner."

"I talked to you this morning. On the phone."

"Then you're Charlie Fentress. In Fred Witherspoon's office. I've heard him speak of you." He leaned across Bill to shake hands.

"Sorry we had to meet like this." Fentress shook hands, sank back. "Taylor was just telling me you and Mister Bedford . . ."

"Anthony Bedford," Dick clarified for him.

Fentress accepted the addition. "You and Anthony Bedford failed to keep an appointment with him this morning. Out at the farm."

"Appointment? This morning?" Dick turned a surprised face down at Bill. "I thought we agreed last night. . ."

"Sure. I know. We weren't going to press him. But this morning when you called up and said he wanted us to go ahead with the project, I thought . . ." Bill's voice died slowly before the frank bewilderment in Dick's face.

"I phoned you?"

"About eight." Bill scowled, remembering. He could hear the phone ringing; it had startled him. "I was in the shower, so it must have been about eight."

"But I was asleep at eight." Dick turned to apologize to Fentress. "Partied too well last night. I overslept, didn't get to the office till nearly ten."

Bill could see the tightening of Fentress' hands across his knees and sensed rather than saw the ripple of muscles across Casey's shoulders. Bill knew what they were thinking.

The phone call that hadn't happened. The first little discrepancy.

Chapter III

"Let's go over that again." Fentress made the request pleasantly, looking straight at Bill. "You had this phone call setting an appointment at the Bedford farm . . ."

Dick thumped himself down on the arm of Bill's chair, his hand still gripping Bill's shoulder firmly. He squeezed reassuringly once and leaned forward. "Let me fill in a little background." Fentress nodded and settled back as Dick went smoothly on. "Anthony Bedford still holds the old family place, though he hasn't farmed it for years. He also has money, a lot of money. Bill and I dreamed up the idea, not new but sound, of a smart, exclusive subdivision, to be built on that land. With Barnes & Taylor doing the building, naturally. We approached Bedford with the plan."

"He was interested?"

"Let's say he was willing to listen. Last night we had a party at my place, just Bill and Penny and Janet and me. Janet's our secretary, Bill's and mine." Dick smiled briefly. "In fact, that's the firm, Janet, Bill and me. The party was to discuss strategy, and we decided then not to press Bedford." He looked down at Bill for confirmation. "Let the idea simmer. What made you think I'd changed my mind overnight, Bill?"

"Because you phoned. You said to meet you and Bedford at the farm." Bill started up, almost knocking Dick off the chair arm. "Excuse me." He glanced down at Fentress. "I just remembered. I don't have to guess what was said. It's written down." He didn't ask permission, just started for the stairs. Casey fell in beside him. Fentress' voice, however, stopped them both.

"If it's written down, one of my men will get it. Where would it be?" Pleasant but firm.

Bill turned back into the room. "The pad on the night table, by the phone." He watched from the archway as Pilsudski—or was it O'Hara?—went stolidly up the stairs.

"Bring the whole pad," Fentress called after him, and then glanced at Bill. "Why should you write it down?"

"Me?" He felt his own astonishment showing. "But I told you I was in the shower. Penny took the call. She always writes down phone messages."

Dick nodded confirmation. "She was in show business, you know. Before she married. Phone calls were important. And correct times and addresses even more so."

"And she'd recognize your voice, Barnes?"

"I should certainly think so. She'd heard it often enough."

"On the phone?"

"Yes. She was always calling the office now, since Bill is outside man, she got me more often than Bill." He knocked a knuckle against his teeth. "Wait! Maybe you misunderstood her. Maybe Bedford set up the date." He sighed with relief. "Sounds more like Bedford, calling at eight. He's an early riser. I'm not."

Bill scowled, trying to remember just what Penny had read so triumphantly from the pad, holding it at arm's length so she could see. She wouldn't wear glasses. He could see her, hugging the pad close and squealing exultantly, "It's set. We're rich!" He was positive she had said Dick had phoned. Not Bedford.

Fentress pinned it down. "We'll know as soon as Pilsudski brings the pad."

As if on cue the policeman clumped down the stairs, clutching the leather-backed pad under his arm like a reluctant schoolboy. He marched across the room to hand it to Fentress and stand guard over it.

Fentress flipped back the cover and riffled through the pages. He looked up at Bill. "It's blank." He said it calmly, as if that was what he had expected to find.

As Bill reached uncertainly for it again Fentress held it delicately by the spine and shook it. A single page fluttered out. He caught it dexterously in midair and glanced at it. He laid the pad on one knee and folded the page once before he handed it to Bill. "You may want that." Casey scowled darkly at the transaction, especially when Bill tucked the paper in his pocket without reading it.

He didn't need to read it. He knew it was one of his sentimental night-notes to Penny. He thanked Fentress with his eyes. Then he began to worry. Why wasn't the other note there? Penny was careful about making phone memos but she wasn't so meticulous about housekeeping that she'd clear the pad. He could remember times when he'd had to rip out whole pages of doodles of long-past and forgotten phone calls to clear a space for his own memos.

"Maybe it's in the wastebasket," he suggested.

"Casey's taken care of the wastebaskets, though your wife seems to have cleaned house pretty thoroughly before it happened."

Bill shook his head. That didn't sound like Penny, who usually left everything for Mrs. Harris, who wasn't due until tomorrow. But Penny had been angry when he left. He had heard, somewhere, that women often worked off their anger in a bout of cleaning house. That would account for her going back to the housecoat, too, after he'd seen her dressed at the window. "How about the trash and garbage cans?" he suggested, and immediately felt foolish.

It wasn't foolish. Fentress nodded solemnly. "Casey's taking care of those, too."

"Routine," Casey croaked his refrain.

For the first time Bill became conscious of activity all around him, quiet, methodical activity. It was beginning to dawn on him that his own private world of grief no longer mattered. This was a "case"; Penny simply a victim, this house the scene of the crime. And I'm a suspect.

Dick's arm slid around his shoulders. "Don't worry, Bill. They'll find the note and that will clear up the whole thing." He turned to Fentress. "I'm sure you'll find it was Bedford who called." He squeezed Bill's shoulders excitedly. "Wait! It could have been Janet, relaying . . . No, she'd have told me when I got in." He nodded decisively. "You'll find it was Bedford." He paused before he said with finality, "Must have been. Nobody knew of the deal but us and the old man."

"We'll check." Fentress nodded to Casey as if to say, "Make a note of that," and Casey looked scornfully back.

Bill sighed and took up his story again. "I went out there and stayed over three hours. I came back and phoned and . . ." He faltered, coughed, remembering with a sudden coldness in his stomach, "and I came home." He let his hands drop between his knees. "That's all I know."

Fentress shook his head. "No, Taylor. You know lots more." Bill jerked his head up to protest and Fentress held up his hand. "You knew Mrs. Taylor. And the victim is the center of the crime. Let's start with Penny. Who was she?"

Who was Penny? How could he tell them? How could he make them see her as a glamorous, gay and lovely woman, when all they'd ever seen was that thing on the kitchen floor, without a face? She was laughter and love, and the miracle of it was that she was his. He looked across at Fentress and said simply, "She was my wife."

Naturally that didn't satisfy Fentress, but he didn't show irritation, just accepted it and nodded. "Now let's get some of her background. How long had you been married?"

"Three months." Was three months all he'd had, all he'd ever have of Penny? All my real living crowded into three short months!

"How about relatives? Her parents, for instance?"

Bill dredged it up mechanically. "Dr. Frank Steadman of Seattle. He died about two years ago. Her mother's been dead some years."

"Any brothers or sisters?"

"There was a brother. He was killed on Iwo Jima."

"Okinawa," Dick corrected, and then apologized. "I understood her to say Okinawa."

"Know his name?" Fentress prodded, ignoring Dick.

"What difference does that . . . Oh, Stan, I think. Stanley Steadman. He was in the Marines."

"Was she well off? Did she have money of her own, I mean?"

"Huh?" Bill had to think that over slowly. He'd first met Penny when he was staying up at Uncle Ralph's lodge at Caswell, and she'd been driving a Cadillac convertible and living at the smartest hotel. But she'd told him the Caddy belonged to a friend, and since she'd been singing at the hotel, naturally she'd stay there. The Caddy had disappeared but that didn't matter, since he had had any of Uncle Ralph's array of cars to choose from. They had used the Rolls roadster and the MG indiscriminately, and once, to go to a formal dance, the big and rather stuffy Daimler, complete with Donny, Uncle Ralph's chauffeur. Bill had proposed to Penny one night in the MG and been accepted the next, after considerable hesitation, in the Rolls. No, the borrowed Caddy didn't argue money. Of course, Penny had had beautiful clothes, especially evening things, but then she was a singer, who'd naturally spend money on clothes. And anyway, he didn't know whether a woman's clothes meant money or simply shrewd shopping. And since their marriage they'd lived on what he had. If Penny had had money he was quite sure she'd have spent it. She loved spending money.

"No, I don't think she had any money. When her father was alive they had plenty. At least I suppose so. She went to Finch's and then Goucher. They're both expensive schools." His voice ran down of its own accord. Thinking of Penny, remembering her bright spates of talk hurt like the very devil. "That's all, I guess."

"What about her friends?"

Bill had to think back. There were names, of course, but mostly names like Jack and Evelyn, Sandra, a Feodor who played divinely, somebody named Kip, and two Helens he always confused, much to Penny's amusement. "They're not at all alike," she'd say, "but I can't always be saying Helen R. or Helen B., now can I, Bill?" There were other names churning around in his head but he couldn't pin them down. Oh, yes, and then just this past week there had been that little flurry of luncheons and bridge-teas, mostly with women he knew—Marge Satterthwaite, Fay Compton, Ella Fields. He offered these to Fentress, not very hopefully, though at the time he'd been grateful to his old friends for taking Penny in. She'd been a little lost here. Oh, yes, and there was one other.

"Phil Cameron. That's the fellow who could tell you more about her. He was manager of the hotel where she sang." And there was somebody else up there—her manager or agent or something. Fulton? No, Folsom. Kenneth Folsom. He told Fentress, "He was her manager."

"Manager? Why did she need a manager?"

"She was a singer." Bill glanced up from his hands in surprise, and then wondered at his own surprise. Of course Fentress hadn't known.

"She had a beautiful voice," Dick contributed. "Low and husky."

Fentress nodded comprehension and turned to Bill. "Know anything about her career? Where she sang? Things like that?"

"Only casually. It was just a pastime with her. You know, the way debutantes take up a career for a while. The smart thing . . ."

"What about dates? Can you pin any of it down?"

Bill scowled, trying to remember. Penny had been so flip about her career, so completely casual, that he hadn't bothered to find out. There was so much else fascinating about her that he was constantly learning new things. Careers and the past could wait until they had settled calmly into marriage and reminiscence. Winter evening stuff. He shook his head. "I'm no help there."

Dick leaned across him, his hand on Bill's knee. "Maybe I can help." He paused, waiting for some indication to go ahead.

Bill thumped his hand lightly. "Anything to help, Dick."

"Well, she was singing at *El Camino,* a sort of night club in Pasadena, back in 1945. During the war. I saw her there."

Fentress focused quickly on Dick. "Then you knew her before Taylor did?"

Bill swiveled his neck around. "I didn't know you'd known Penny."

Dick squeezed Bill's shoulder, but he addressed Fentress. "I could hardly say I knew her. I heard her sing there, once. I was stationed near by. We had special liberty one night and we made it special, so I wasn't in any condition to remember her."

Bill nodded. . . . "I remember. You were telling about that week-end."

Dick explained to Fentress, "It was my Big Moment. My war career, you might say. We were going overseas the next week, only the war ended. Everybody has one war story. That's mine. The weekend." Dick whistled softly. "They tell me I tried to fly a streetcar."

Bill clutched at it. Every memory of Penny was precious now. He could remember Penny pouting because Dick hadn't remembered her. Most men did. "Penny had to remind him he must have seen her."

"If I did, she'd have looked like a chorus line. I was seeing triple." He patted Bill's shoulder. To Fentress he said, "That's little enough, but it's a date."

"It gives us a starting point. *El Camino,* Pasadena, the week before VJ day. That would be around early July, 1945." Fentress aimed that directly at Pilsudski, and for the first time Bill realized all this was being taken down.

Bill fought down an impulse to yell at Fentress to leave and take his blasted policemen with him. That would be stupid and worse than useless. Only through Fentress and his men would he find the man who had killed Penny. If it was somebody from her past, then he'd tear that past to shreds trying to find him. Suddenly he realized Fentress had asked a question. He raised his head. "What was that?"

"What name did she use?"

"Name? Oh, as a singer, you mean? Penny Wise."

"Steadman. Penny Steadman. What name did she marry under?"

Suddenly Bill felt uncomfortable. It had always made him uneasy, as if the marriage weren't quite legal, so he blurted it out, "Penny Wise." He slowed down after that, explaining, "That was the way she wanted it. She said she'd been using it so long anything else felt silly."

Fentress accepted that calmly, "Many professional people take their stage names legally."

Fentress rose and began saying goodbye, while Casey gathered up his men, herding them out.

Chapter IV

Gradually Bill became conscious of the immense, hearse-like car drawn up behind his own Chewy and determinedly avoided looking at it, not permitting his mind to know what it was. Penny, who had loved bright green convertibles, was to ride in that. Then full realization hit him and he backed away from the window, his eyes swinging to the huge car. In its way it was as impressive as Uncle Ralph's huge and stuffy Daimler, but the Daimler was at least new. This car was an elderly and outmoded Packard, yet all its metal twinkled and its point gleamed, like a living travesty on an ancient ad seen in *The National Geographic* in a dentist's office. It was an immense limousine, as rigid and uncompromising as a shoebox, with enough gleaming windows to make it seem a rolling hothouse. And there was only one person who would be seen in such a monstrosity—Miss Emily Cole, who, in her way, was as outmoded, as impressive and as immense as the car.

Bailey, her chauffeur, dismounted. There was no other word for it except "dismounted." He got out of the car as if it were a skittish horse, as if thirty years of driving it had not yet convinced him it wouldn't shy or bolt. Beside the high, squarish car he seemed even smaller than he was, and he was a small man, a man who looked as if he might have been a jockey and probably had been, back in

the days when the Coles had raced their blooded horses at
Epsom Downs and Lawrenceville. He opened the rear door
and stepped away from the rush. Miss Emily hurtled out
of the car as if confinement even in that spacious vehicle
had been too much for her. Her rush carried her halfway
across the sidewalk before she braked her charge with a
silver- knobbed walking stick and looked up at the house.
She turned back to Bailey and issued brief orders in a
voice that must have been clearly audible in the open, four
blocks away. Bill could even hear the rumble of authority
through his window.

He watched her shake herself more solidly into her gray
suit that gave her the appearance of a battleship in "moth-
balls," and then she started toward the house.

"Oh, no!" It was, he realized, a futile protest. Nothing
stopped the avalanche of Miss Emily's progress. If she was
going to offer sympathy, however inappropriate the time
or unwanted the sympathy, she was going to do it.

When he flung open the front door he discovered he
wasn't going to get sympathy.

"Bill, I'm a fool!"

Miss Emily slammed past him like a tank in full charge,
her beads clanking, her heavy tread thudding through the
house, her silver-knobbed walking stick pounding an off-
beat rhythm to her clomping. She passed with such swift
and overpowering majesty that Bill was still holding open
the door and staring into the street when she bellowed
again from the living room.

"Stop gawping and come here."

"Yes ma'am." Obediently Bill shut the door and followed her dazedly into the living room, where she was
already testily poking at the big overstuffed chair with her
stick. She swiveled in a mastodon parody of a ballet and
let go, her bulk hurtling into the chair with a whoosh that
made Bill wince.

"Sit down! Sit down!" Miss Emily gestured so fiercely her stick threatened the table lamp. Then she dropped it at her side, cupping one massive freckled hand over the knob. "On second thought, keep standing up. You're the only man I know who's big enough to make me feel dainty." Her deep, resonant voice suddenly went plaintive. "And, Bill, right now I need to feel dainty. I want to feel helpless and small and forgivable, when I know I really need to have my behind kicked." Startling blue eyes peered up at him from the brown, wrinkled face, eyes that were disconcertingly pleading. "Can you forgive me, Bill?"

Bill sat down slowly, knowing his mind wasn't functioning clearly right now. "Forgive you, Miss Emily. For what?"

"I told the police." For Miss Emily, her voice was small and apologetic. "I sent them here."

"Oh!"

"Oh, what?" Miss Emily's voice regained some of its command.

"Just oh." He woke up then. "Oh, yes. I see. I hadn't even gotten around to wondering how they knew. But of course somebody had to tell them. Don't feel bad about it."

Miss Emily regarded him for a long moment, both hands clasped over the silver knob of her stick, one of her several chins resting on her hands. Finally she sighed and sat back in the chair.

"You didn't kill her, did you?" It wasn't a question, just a statement that invited corroboration.

Bill shook his head. "How did you know?"

Miss Emily blinked, stared at Bill, shook herself janglingly.

"The little fool invited me to dinner."

"Huh?" The complete non-sequitur baffled him, left him feeling that he had swung at a punching bag and hit a feather pillow.

"Nobody invites me to dinner. Not these days, with steak the price it is, and the way I eat. So naturally I thought it was a gag. Especially when she started screaming."

"You heard her? Screaming? When? Where?" Bill stood up, glaring down at Miss Emily, pounding his fist on the arm of her chair in cadence to his words. "Where? When?"

Miss Emily drew back, snorting. "On the phone. At eleven-thirty. At my house. At least I was at my house."

"Penny phoned you?"

"To invite me to dinner. Tomorrow night! As if I wouldn't have my calendar set for a week at least." For a moment Miss Emily seemed to brood over this social faux pas; then she shivered, remembering. "Then she started screaming."

"You actually heard her!" Bill pressed his fist across his eyes, as if that would shut out the picture he was seeing.

"Bill . . ." Miss Emily's voice was pleading for understanding, and yet there was bafflement in it, as if she didn't understand her own words or quite what they were saying. "It sounded so melodramatic I was sure it was a gag. And if it was, I was going to play along. So I called the police. Bill, I didn't dream . . ." Her big old hand clamped down on his harshly.

"Of course you didn't, Miss Emily. Did you tell them what she said?" He felt the dryness of her skin as she withdrew her hand. He saw her eyes go bleak, as if she were hiding something. "You didn't tell them everything!"

"I just said there was trouble at your house and to get there in a hurry."

"But she did say something. I know she did." He tugged at the vast immobility of Miss Emily. "You've got to tell the police just what she said. Everything. There might be a clue in it,"

"You wouldn't want me to, Bill." It was flat and final. So flat and so final Bill stopped tugging and just looked at her. He knew what she was going to say and yet he had to hear her say it.

"You can't stop there, Miss Emily."

Miss Emily started picking at the immense string of gold balls that looped twice around her neck and hung over her vast bosom to end in a medallion that could have served as a wall plaque. "You understand, Bill, the girl was talking about you, thinking about you, when it happened. . . ." You don't have to explain Penny to me, he wanted to scream at her. "And right in the middle of saying she wouldn't take 'No' for an answer she sort of laughed and said, 'Oh, here comes Bill now, sneaking in the back door.'"

"You're sure she said the 'back door'? I almost never use it."

"Yes, back door. Then I heard her—well, it was as if she turned away to call you. And then . . ." Miss Emily stopped, one rough dry hand shuffling over the beads tinkingly.

"Go on," he prompted, sick with what he knew was coming. Miss Emily had heard Penny die.

"And then . . . this was all a little off the phone and not all clear, Bill, so I could be mistaken."

"But you know you're not."

"No, I'm not." That seemed to give Miss Emily the impetus she needed to finish. "Penny said, 'Bill, put down that candlestick. Put it down. Have you gone crazy?' And then she screamed. The phone banged around crazily and then somebody hung it up." For a moment Miss Emily brooded on what she had said and then thumped her cane. "Like that movie about the woman on the telephone. That 'Sorry, Wrong Number.' Saw it last week. That's what made me think the call was a gag. Candlestick! Whoever heard . . ."

"Penny was killed with a candlestick. The brass one Uncle Ralph gave us." He stared at the blank space on the mantle where it had stood. "She never did like it much," he said irrelevantly, his mind seeing the horrible pictures conjured up by Miss Emily. Then the pictures shifted, the words had new meaning, new and terrible importance. He swung around and dashed out of the room to confirm this new, important knowledge of his. He could hear Miss Emily rumbling to her feet and coming toward the hall. He went past the telephone with only a shivery glance and pushed through the swinging door to the kitchen. Then he turned back, standing in the doorway, his big frame silhouetted against the bright kitchen, his face shadowed by the darkened hall.

Miss Emily stepped briskly into the hall and came to a dead halt, her stick skidding on the polished floor. "Omigawd, Bill! She couldn't see the face!" Miss Emily's big voice whimpered off into relief. "She couldn't see the face! So it doesn't make any difference what she said."

Bill came forward then, feeling for the first time that there was something alive inside him, that the world outside still lived, and the two had somehow made contact. "You've got to tell them what she said. Every word of it. Don't you see?"

"Nonsense. They know she's dead. They know the candlestick killed her. The only additional thing I could tell 'em would make 'em suspect you. The fools!"

Bill brushed that aside. "The important thing is size."

It was Miss Emily's turn to look blank. "Size?"

"I'm big, Miss Emily. So're you. We're both used to being big so we don't notice it. But other people do. Penny said if she missed me, she just looked for the biggest man in the crowd and there I was. She was always conscious of how big I was. Because she was so small."

Miss Emily was already nodding. She had seen the same thing he had. "She couldn't see his face but she could see size. He must have been as big as you, Bill. Or nearly."

"So you've got to tell Fentress."

Miss Emily reared back mulishly at being told she had to do something, even something she herself knew she ought to do. Then she studied Bill's face and sighed gustily. "You're a fool, Bill. Or naive as a babe. Or both. Or shrewder than one man has a right to be. Oh, come on." She thudded down the hall, muttering. "If you didn't kill her, it's the right thing to do. And if you did, it's a smart thing to do." She chuckled deep and rumbling. "I've always liked you. Bill—but not for your brains. And if you ask me, that's a helluva reason for believing a man didn't murder his wife. Because you think he wasn't smart enough to."

Bill, gave up any pretense of courteously escorting Miss Emily and simply saved his energies for catching up with her. At the curb Bailey already had the car door open and had stepped back out of range of Miss Emily's charge. She banged through the door and lurched into the saggiest part of the seat in one furious motion. She pounded on the seat beside her, yelling for Bill to get in, at the same time giving Bailey specific directions for getting to the courthouse.

Once the car was in motion and Miss Emily was relatively quiet, Bill asked her what she meant—that he wasn't smart enough. "I've got an alibi based on a memorandum that doesn't exist of a phone call that wasn't made for an appointment nobody ever heard of."

"I know, Bill. I got the outlines from the local newscast."

"So how could that be smart?"

"Because no man in his right mind would tell that story and expect to be believed. This way, it's just screwy enough to be real."

"It's real all right. I just can't understand what happened to the memo. Penny never bothers much about cleaning up, so I can't figure out why she bothered to throw it away."

"Maybe she didn't." Miss Emily swiveled her head around, so that Bill could feel her eyes studying him. "Had you thought of that?"

"Then who did?"

"The murderer."

"That's crazy." Even as he said it Bill could feel his throat go dry, feel a tightening in his stomach that was the beginning of fear. "Why would he do that?"

"To destroy your alibi."

"But how would he know about that memo?" And as he asked the question he knew the answer. He didn't need Miss Emily's husky words to tell him.

"Because he made that phone call."

"I was just waking up to that, Miss Emily." He licked suddenly dry lips. "That means he planned to kill her, planned to get me out of the house."

"And planned to destroy your alibi, Bill."

"But why?"

"Somebody means for you to hang for this murder, Bill."

Chapter V

"Bill, I'm scared. And when I'm scared, I'm scared all over—and there's an awful lot of me."

"What are you scared of?"

"Maybe we're doing just what he wants us to do, reporting that phone call."

"That's crazy! That's the one thing he couldn't have planned—Penny talking to you just as he walked in. Her mistaking him for me was just his fool's luck. Only it might not be. That's what I'm banking on. It's a clue to his size." Bill locked his big knuckles and stared at them. "Our only clue, so far as I can see."

Miss Emily shook her head so violently her beads rippled in tinkling protest and then she sank back, brooding darkly, so that for several blocks she forgot to yell traffic directions at Bailey and didn't even put much heart into it when she told him to park in the spot specifically marked for the Mayor's car.

Bill was so preoccupied he missed noticing that Miss Emily didn't leave the car with her usual rhinoceros charge but got out heavily, even wearily, as if she felt her sixty-five years and two hundred and fifty pounds.

Inside the porticoed building, Bill, searching for Fentress' office, peered down the dim vastness of vaulted corridors that suggested incense and sanctity and smelled of cleaning compound and leaky steam radiators. Casey rolled out of a side corridor, swung toward them in a wide sweep. At the top of his arc he whispered hoarsely to Bill, "Been looking for you," and started back, doing his best to ignore Miss Emily. It was, at best, a wistfully hopeless gesture. Miss Emily went right along with them. They got her seated in the largest chair of an anteroom and Casey said soothingly, "It's just that the loot has come up with some new questions."

"Should try coming up with a few answers, to my way of thinking. I'll wait—" Miss Emily pawed angrily across her vast bosom and finally located a dangling lapel watch which she studied belligerently—"ten minutes."

Casey nodded and led the way to Fentress' inner office, a large, neat room with a desk angled into a corner between two windows. Subconsciously Bill noted the stratagem. Fentress' face and expressions would be almost unreadable with the light behind him, while his visitor's would be exposed mercilessly. Bill sat where Fentress indicated. "I've got some information. I brought along . . ."

"Miss Emily Cole," Casey finished for him with a sigh.

Fentress, in his darkened corner, nodded pleasantly. "Oh, yes. She gave us the information about . . . Yes, Mrs. Frederic Tilworthy."

Bill blinked. Miss Emily had been an institution for so long that he had forgotten she was once married and had two children. Mr. Frederic Tilworthy wasn't even a memory, but Bill could recall the children, a daughter who had married and moved away and a younger son, Freddy Junior, about whom he'd heard hints of a tragedy that Miss Emily never discussed. The sudden stopping of Fentress' easy, pleasant voice recalled him. He looked up. "I beg your pardon?"

"I said," Fentress began as if he didn't mind repeating, "That the police of Seattle tell us no Doctor Frank Steadman ever practiced there."

"I'm sure she said Seattle." Bill puzzled it over. "Yes, Seattle. We used to talk about the steep streets and . . ." He stopped, hurt by the sudden recollection that he would never again talk with Penny. He managed to say with dignity, "There must be some mistake."

"Nor any birth certificate for a female Steadman of her age."

"Good Lord, Fentress, Penny could have been any where between twenty-four and twenty-eight or so. She was . . ." He couldn't describe Penny. He caught himself up sharply. "You couldn't have checked all possible dates."

"Her marriage certificate gave her birth date as July 21, 1925. That's quite specific. And in her own handwriting."

"Oh, I see. Yes." It was automatic agreement. Bill was trying to clarify a picture of Penny—for himself, for Fentress. "She was glamorous, you know. And beautiful. And a singer. Maybe she felt—I can see where an actress might feel that a doctor was a more glamorous father than—oh, say, a truck driver."

"Unfortunately for that theory, Taylor, birth certificates are unrelated to future glamour. Truck drivers' children also have them."

Bill caught the sarcasm in Fentress' words, though the voice was amiably noncommittal. He flushed and stared at the square, uncompromising feet of the desk. "She made up her stage name, Penny Wise." He looked up quickly. "Or did she? Was Wise her real name?"

"We tried Seattle on 'Wise,' too."

"Of course you would." Bill studied the neat pile of papers on the desk and spoke to them rather than Fentress. "Maybe she made up her past, too."

"And maybe she ain't the one made it up," Casey commented darkly to a sparrow on the window ledge, so that for the first time Bill was conscious he had remained in the room.

He ignored Casey's implication and went on talking to the papers on the desk. "Stage people do," Bill defended her, "to add glamour. Not that there's anything wrong with their pasts. They just—well, dramatize a little."

"All of us do, to some extent," Fentress agreed, and then sighed. "So that's all you can tell us? Well, we can get at her past through her fingerprints. As an entertainer she probably registered with U.S.O. or Theater Wing. They all required fingerprint registration."

"Look," Bill knotted his big hands painfully, "if Penny had something in her past that she glamorized, can't we leave it at that? Maybe her father was the town drunk, for all I know. Why dig up something she wanted hidden, something probably innocent, but disillusioning?"

"You know better than that," Fentress chided. "If your story is to stand up, it must have been someone from her past who killed her. And according to your story—" He referred to a typed sheet on his desk—"you met Miss Wise in Caswell, went with her two weeks, married her, honeymooned for three weeks, and she's been in town only about nine weeks. Now, according to your story, she met almost no one. . . ."

"Good Lord, Fentress, you can't make anything of our seclusion. We'd just been married. We wanted to be alone."

"My understanding precisely." Fentress laid down the paper very carefully in the center of his desk. "Would you have me believe that a charming girl like your wife had made such a violent enemy in such a short time? Do you want me to believe that one of that very limited circle of friends . . ."

"No! Of course not!" Bill stopped him roughly and then sat back. "Sorry. I see your point."

Fentress picked up another paper and appeared to read it, but Bill suspected he knew its contents verbatim. He laid it down, held it smooth with spread hand. "How did you feel about the baby?"

The shift caught him unawares. "Baby? You did say baby, didn't you?" As Fentress nodded Bill rubbed a knuckle across the ridge of his brows. "What baby?"

"Your wife's. You didn't tell me she was pregnant."

"She wasn't. She didn't want children. Not right away."

"Fight over it?" Casey croaked from the window ledge where he sat rocking on a fat hip. A small dark man had come in to stand near him.

"Of course not. We talked it over like civilized people and decided we'd wait. Until the firm was making more money."

Fentress' sleek head bent over the paper, then turned politely to Bill. "The autopsy report shows she was pregnant."

"That's impossible! A husband would know."

Fentress glanced inquiringly at the little dark man who shook his head. Fentress swung back to Bill. "Doctor Flournoy, our medical examiner, doesn't agree with you."

The doctor spoke with careful, classroom deliberation. "Mrs. Taylor was four and a half months pregnant."

Dully Bill heard himself say, "That's crazy."

"The foetus was quite well defined. The skeletal structure . . ."

The medical examiner was describing, with some relish, his precise findings when Bill came out of his chair, fists on Fentress' desk to control their shaking.

"You're a liar!"

He could feel himself shouting, feel the rasp of words in his throat without really hearing them. These men were saying that Penny— He sat down abruptly. "Oh, don't worry. I'm not going to strangle him."

"No?" Casey had moved up beside his chair expectantly.

"You're a violent man, Taylor." Fentress teetered back in his chair, poised, waiting. Suddenly chair legs crashed to the floor and he became suave again, quiet. "Then I can assume you didn't know of this pregnancy?"

"You can assume to hell-and-gone. It isn't true."

Casey leaned down, mouth close to his ear. "Did you kill her when you found out?"

Fentress' quiet voice cut across Casey's. "You've only known her a little over three months."

"Did she make you marry her?"

". . . And yet she was four and half months pregnant. . . ."

"When you found out, did you grab a candlestick and . . ."

Bill deliberately shut his mind to the hammering words, to Casey's deep, hoarse voice, to Fentress, casual, polite, even helpful. They were badgering him. They wanted him to leap from his chair and grab something, flail out at them. Instead he sat tight, his big hands crunching down on his thighs until his bones ached. He didn't speak until he was sure he could control his voice, and then he said, very quietly, "Stop."

The voices lopped off into silence that hurt for a moment. Bill spoke quietly, weighing his words and testing his ability to say them. "If this is some sort of psychological third degree, it isn't going to work. Just ask me, and I'll tell you. I didn't know Penny was pregnant. I'm not sure of it now. There may be some mistake. The wrong report, or the wrong tests. . . ."

Fentress shook his head. "We make mistakes but not like that."

The quiet assurance of the man's words ripped through Bill more than the hammering phrases of a moment ago. These men had taken Penny from his home, borne her out physically, and now they were giving her back to him piecemeal, but a Penny he didn't know, couldn't recognize, a Penny who lied about her name, her childhood, a Penny who married him while carrying another man's child.

Suddenly the outer door burst violently in and Miss Emily roared through, flinging off a girl who clung to her arm.

"I said ten minutes, and thundering wallupuses, I'm going in!"

Even Casey backed away from her lumbering assault, and the doctor scurried for a seat in the far window sill, out of range of Miss Emily's charging wrath. Miss Emily braked herself with her stick directly in front of Fentress' glass-topped desk and glared. "That young idiot wants me to tell you about the telephone call his wife made. I think it's a fool thing to do. I think it may hang him. He doesn't. And it's his neck he's risking, so I'll tell you. . . ." And Miss Emily told them, tapping out her points with the silver knob of her stick on the glass top of Fentress' desk.

Aside from wincing slightly with each tap, Fentress listened politely until Miss Emily thumped an accompaniment to, "So you can look for a big man, like one of your goons."

"Miss Emily," Fentress laid his hands flat on the desk, thumbs hooked over the edge, as if he were about to rise and excuse himself, "I can see why Bill Taylor might want you to tell me this story, even though it seems damnably incriminating." He pushed himself up, almost erect, leaning across the desk to peer at Miss Emily. "But I should like to know your motive for bringing me any such fantastic story. It's impossible, medically impossible, for Mrs. Taylor to have made any such phone call. Penny Taylor was unconscious for more than half an hour before she was attacked. She was already dying. She had been poisoned."

They both held the pose, glaring across the desk, Fentress leaning stiffly on tented fingers, Miss Emily holding her stick high like a standard.

"And since Mrs. Taylor could not have made any such call, Miss Emily, how did you happen to know enough to inform the police of her murder?"

Miss Emily's stick whipped down, the knob crashed into the glass desk top. A star pattern splintered in the glass.

Chapter VI

Bill stared at the star frosted into the glass desk top and tried to assimilate what had been said, test it for implications. First, of course, there was a surge of relief, however grim. Penny had been unconscious, dying; she had not felt those brutal, mangling blows. Then he swallowed with revulsion. Someone must have hated her, to have beaten her like that when he must have known she was already dying. Some former suitor, maybe insanely jealous that Bill had won what he had lost? Yes, he could accept that. And then he remembered the medical evidence. Some man had loved Penny, been loved, and there was going to be a child. Would the father . . .

Miss Emily was roaring, "And if you think I'm going to pay for your blasted desk top, you're mistaken. I pay enough taxes already. Silly idea having glass on a desk top, anyway. Honest wood's good enough. Better." She paused for breath and a shift of attack. "Well, young man, are you going to make anything of that phone call? I got it, you know."

Fentress shut his eyes and leaned hard on his hands. His lips moved stiffly as if he might be praying. Bill didn't think he was. Finally he sat down wearily. "Make anything of it? Miss Emily, I only wish I could." He studied some papers on his desk and looked up again. "How long after you received this call did you phone the police?"

"Immediately. Maybe three minutes. Talked to a desk sergeant here. I was very brief. I always am when I'm angry."

Fentress rubbed away a half-smile. "Almost too brief. According to this report, filed at eleven thirty-five, you only said, 'There's trouble at Bill Taylor's on Morningside Road,' and hung up. It took us," he consulted a paper, "two minutes to look up the address and six minutes more to get a radio car to the house. The medical examiner was there in another ten minutes. He specifies she had been dead approximately an hour."

"Give or take ten minutes," Flournoy spoke from his scrunched position on the window seat, his hands hugging his thin, bony knees.

"That puts the bludgeoning at around ten-thirty . . ."

"Give or take ten minutes," the doctor repeated.

Miss Emily batted her chin lightly with the silver knob. "Long before I got the call."

"And she was unconscious before that. At least half an hour."

"Chloral hydrate. Nearly a gram. Administered thirty to forty minutes prior to death. Must have put her out like a light." Flournoy snapped his fingers, glanced over at Bill and hastily wrapped his arms around his knees again. "It was in the Scotch," he added.

"So from about ten o'clock on, Mrs. Taylor was incapable of making *any* telephone calls."

"She made one to me." Miss Emily was even more impressive because now there was no bluster, no waving stick, no shouted words.

"Miss Emily," Fentress was wearily patient, "We've just proved that it was impossible. Do you still expect me to believe it?"

"You can believe six impossible things before breakfast, if you try hard enough," Miss Emily misquoted.

"This is not Wonderland, Miss Emily, and it's not before breakfast. This is the courthouse, and it's after lunch." He glanced at his wrist watch in surprise. "Long after lunch. That is, everybody else's lunch. I haven't had time for one." He lowered his head briefly on his hands, sighed and looked up. "And I'm not likely to get one. Now, Miss Emily, about this call you say you got . . ."

"I got it."

"But are you positive it was Mrs. Taylor talking?"

Miss Emily's mouth worked, as if she were reciting what she had heard on the phone. Suddenly her eyes glinted balefully. "If it wasn't, it was someone who knew . . ." She thumped her stick angrily.

"Knew what?" Fentress prompted.

"Huh?" Miss Emily looked vaguely at him. "I was just thinking it had to be someone who knew us both fairly well. But it was nothing a woman who knew Penny well enough to imitate her voice might not know. Just a remark about a previous meeting. Nothing, really." Miss Emily being airily nonchalant had the subtlety of a playful rhinoceros. It didn't deceive Bill and he was certain it hadn't deceived Fentress.

Miss Emily was lying.

Fentress, however, seemed perfectly willing to slide over that point. "But now that you know it couldn't have been Mrs. Taylor, do you think you might identify the caller as someone you know?"

"I accepted the call as genuine. As far as I am concerned, it was Penny talking." Miss Emily was still struggling with some other thoughts. Her mind was on Fentress' question only by compulsion. She sighed gustily. "So I can't help."

Fentress seemed unconcerned. "By the time we're ready for a formal statement perhaps you'll recall what it is that now bothers you subconsciously about that call." He hadn't forgotten Miss Emily had lied. She glared at him, nodded and pivoted on her stick to face Bill. "Don't seem to have done you much good."

"On the contrary," Fentress put in smoothly, "if that call were genuine it certainly tended to incriminate Taylor. Let's say it was intended to incriminate him. But that backfires once we know the call was fabricated." He hesitated and stared directly at Miss Emily. "Even if you fabricated it."

Miss Emily's ample chest swelled and her mouth opened for a roar from which Fentress was already prepared to cringe. Instead of bellowing, she laughed. "Charles, you don't mind saying what you think. I'll pay for that desk top. Cash." Miss Emily dived into her purse. In the midst of her scrabble she looked up. "I take it Bill walks out of here with me."

"I'm not an arresting officer. You'll have to take that up with Casey. However, I think . . ."

"What the loot thinks, I gotta think," Casey croaked. He looked Bill over for a dark and dubious moment. "But when it comes time to do, I do the doing."

"Fair division of labor," Miss Emily approved, and hunched over the shattered desk to write out a check, het back as level and solid as a baby flattop.

The door burst open and Dick Barnes, looking flushed and angry, strode in, followed more decorously by paunchy, dapper Felix Whitsell, the firm's attorney. Dick came up beside Bill's chair, dropping a hand on his shoulder. "Don't worry. Felix will get you out, if he has to get a habeas corpus. Judge Linkleiter will . . ."

"But I'm not in. Not in that sense, anyway." Bill grinned up at his partner, mildly astonished at the idea of Dick being impetuous and protective. "Miss Emily just came down to give some evidence."

"Oh!" Momentarily Dick looked like a small boy whose firecracker had developed a wet fuse; then he smiled and clapped Bill on the back. "Great. Wonderful. Maybe that will clear things up." He sighted down the flight-deck of Miss Emily's back and nodded to Fentress.

Introductions were made around casually, and even Bill watched with curious detachment. Dick flung himself on the arm of the chair. Bill tugged at Dick's sleeve. "How did you know I was here?"

"From Janet. They had her down here about that Bedford call. She knew nothing of it, of course." He leaned down confidentially. "And while she was down here I had her look up the files on the Bedford place. With this in the papers, the secret is out, so we might as well push it for all it's worth now, before competitors get at him."

Business as usual. He hadn't thought that of Dick, and then, with his partner's next words, he was ashamed of his thought.

"Besides, if we don't press hard that alibi of yours might not look so good. You laid it on pretty thick about how important that appointment was." He nodded obliquely at Fentress. "Did he get tough?"

"No. Except on some questions I don't have answers for. Fentress seems eminently fair. It's Casey I'm scared of."

"You're wrong, Bill. Casey only wants an arrest, Fentress wants a case. And he'll worry it until he has one. He's one of those give-'em-enough-rope boys. He likes his facts nailed down."

Fentress was nailing down his facts. Even while he played host he was excusing himself from time to time to take phone calls, to which he made only monosyllabic answers. "Yes. No?" and once, "Check that." It was a slow, dull process until suddenly drama erupted from the phone. "Bring her in," Fentress barked so sharply that Bill turned toward him, sensing his tension, following his eyes to the door. The woman who flounced through, throwing off the hand of an escorting policeman, was so flamboyant she was a caricature—a roadshow Mae West. And her voice was third-string Mae West, too self-consciously ripe and fruity. She paused, touched her hair and smiled around the room.

"If I'da knowed it was a production, I'da wore tights."

The woman so obviously expected all attention that Bill almost missed the tiny, pert redhead who sidled into the room behind the policeman.

Fentress let his lean face twitch once in the beginning of a grin and then stepped forward. "Miss Belle Forbes," he introduced her to the room with a sweeping gesture that almost matched her entrance.

Miss Forbes swayed deeper into the room, facing cruelly into the late afternoon sun. She wasn't nearly as young as she hoped she looked, and her near-mink stole became shoddy rabbit. With one hand pressed under her bulging bosom, she spoke huskily to Fentress. "I was asked to come here and confront the brute who killed my beloved Penny. . . ." She produced a scarf-sized handkerchief from her bosom in one long tugging motion and dabbed at her eyes. "I saw her poor arms, beaten and bruised, heard her whimper with pain, that night she visited me . . ."

"What night was that?"

Miss Forbes didn't relish this interruption of her art but she gave him, petulantly, "Friday. Last Friday." She drew a deep breath that threatened all her zippers and reverted to tragedy. "I want to see the beast who did that to my precious Penny hanged!" She whirled dramatically away from the desk and faced the room. "I do not hesitate to confront him. I defy him. I point out the villain!" Miss Forbes plunged one finger forward theatrically. "I can see

villainy in his face." She was pointing directly at an astonished Casey.

"God, you're hamming it, Sadie." It was the pert little
red-head. "And anyway, you're pointing at the wrong guy.
Can't you see he's a cop?"

"Not without my glasses," Miss Forbes said with hoarse,
bitter honesty.

Chapter VII

Despite the gravity of the woman's charge, Bill had to stifle a wild impulse to laugh.

Belle twitched her stole petulantly and peered at the redhead. "And my name ain't Sadie. Not any more. It's Belle—Belle Forbes."

"Like mine's Candy Kane," the redhead grinned. "Just tell 'em, Belle, and forget you once read for 'Camille.'"

"I'da got the part, too, if it wasn't for that . . ."

Fentress cut in hastily. "You said you knew the murderer, Miss Forbes," he reminded her.

Belle Forbes grabbed again for the limelight as if it were a tangible thing she could clasp to her bulging bosom.

"I do."

She checked her audience with an eye accustomed to counting the house. Apparently satisfied, she aimed myopic eyes at Fentress and dropped her voice to a husky, conspiratorial whisper well projected for the gallery. "She told me so, with her own lips. She knew death was coming. She had seen his horrible face."

"Whose?"

Fentress' sharp precision rocked her for an instant, But she held tight to her moment of drama, wrapping herself in her stole like a tent-show Sadie Thompson.

"William Carey Taylor."

"What!" The word seemed to lift Fentress half across his desk. "Say that again."

"William Carey Taylor," she repeated, happy in her effect.

Bill heard it, but even repetition didn't make it his name. He wasted a moment trying to pin an identity to it. Fentress, on the other hand, seemed shaken. He had to fumble his way around his desk. "Penny Taylor told you she was afraid of her husband?"

"Wouldn't you be if the guy beat you up?" She tilted her chin haughtily. "Even if he is a rich millionaire, he beat her up."

It wasn't happening. This frowsy, overblown, brassy blonde wasn't saying he had beaten Penny. Without conscious effort he whipped out of his chair and was towering over her, groping for words that would wipe out what she had said.

Belle pouted up at him, her cartwheel hat tilted perilously. "My, you're big." She fingered his arm coyly. "Now a guy like you—"

Fentress pushed between them. "Miss Forbes, that's the man you just called a murderer."

Belle squealed unrealistically and swayed.

"Don't faint here. The floor is hard." Fentress swung to face Bill, ignoring the woman's glare. "And you, Taylor, sit down." He passed over Felix, who had somehow managed to make his chair by the desk a strictly spectator seat, glared at Miss Emily as if daring her to speak, and finally scowled at the policeman who had brought Belle in. "I had no idea her testimony would be so sensational."

The cop was apologetic. "We heard she had some evidence when we was down at The Rendezvous to pick up Cameron and Folsom."

"Ken?" The redhead looked surprised. "Why look for Ken Folsom at our place? He has a variety of interests."

Her scorn made those interests sound illegal and repulsive. "As even a blind cop should know."

The heckled policeman flushed, stammered. Fentress answered for him smoothly. "We may suspect some of his activities, but unfortunately evidence is unavailable. If you'd care to testify . . ." He left the question insinuatingly open. Instead of being offended, the redhead grinned, wet her finger with the tip of her tongue and marked up an invisible score.

"So he's a heel. But he never got much change out of The Rendezvous. The girls know him, and Ben Jade doesn't let him hang around."

"He was around today," Fentress pointed out, consulting a report. "All morning—for a rehearsal."

The redhead nodded offhand agreement. "Trying to explain why one of his fillies didn't show up and pushing a new babe whose ancestors, so he claimed, came over on The Mayflower. Looking her over, I figured she came over on it herself." She thought that over and conceded reluctantly, "But maybe as a young girl."

As upset as he was, Bill smiled and Dick almost choked in his efforts to remain sedate. Miss Emily frankly guffawed and Fentress chuckled before he resumed with the cop.

"Wasn't Cameron there either?"

"Nah. Folsom had been there, like in the report," he stabbed a blunt finger at a paper on the desk, "from ten to after one. But we heard this dame—" he aimed a thumb over his shoulder without looking—"had some dope on the killer, so we brought her in." He glanced uneasily at the redhead. "And she come along."

Fentress' eyes slid past the redhead to the blowzy blonde. "Miss Forbes, do I understand you correctly? Penny Taylor told you her husband physically manhandled her?"

"Huh?" The blonde mumbled "manhandled" a couple of times as if suspicious it was a dirty word; then she brightened. "He beat her up. Regular."

Bill felt an angry, bewildered protest rising, but Fentress cut that off with, "And she was afraid for her life?"

"Terrified." Belle peered nearsightedly around until she located Bill's bulk. "Of him." She aimed a forefinger, thought better of it and pointed her pinky elegantly. "She was backstage to talk over old times."

"Then you've known Mrs. Taylor a long time?"

"Years." Belle waved one hand airily.

"What was her name?"

Belle stared blankly. "You nuts? Mrs. William Carey Taylor. And she had her lines to prove it." This seemed a matter of pride to Belle, actually acquiring a marriage certificate. "Oh, I get you. It was Penny Wise."

"Not her stage name; her real name."

Belle bridled. "Us girls gotta get glamorous names. How'd you like to be called Sadie Glutzman? You'd never get to see a name like that in lights." She neglected to say she had never seen "Belle Forbes," in lights either.

"You have a point. But as an old friend, could you tell us Penny's real name?"

"Suppose it had been Glutzman." Belle clung to an old grievance against her parents.

"Was it?"

Belle sighed with exasperation. "Far's I know it was Wise. Penny Wise. I never heard different."

"You never knew her to use the name Steadman?" Belle glanced uneasily at the redhead, who shook her head slowly. Belle sighed. "Nup. Nor any other." She peered again at the redhead for confirmation, but she wasn't passing any more signals.

Fentress sighed at a promising lead gone. "When was the last time you saw Penny Taylor?"

Without actually counting on her fingers Belle somehow gave that impression. "Friday," she finally announced as a minor triumph.

"And she told you her husband had beaten her? And she was afraid for her life? Just like that?"

Belle looked hurt. "She come in my dressing room for a chat, see. Just among us girls. I guess she was kinda fed up with society and wanted to talk show business."

Society? Bill thought back. Aside from the monthly dances at the country club, two or three little parties Janet had arranged, a few evenings at Dick's and the recent spate of luncheons, there hadn't been much. He sighed. Perhaps the gay and glamorous Penny had found it dull.

Belle minced forward, and half squatted in midair, her hindquarters wriggling. "When she sat down I see she ain't comfortable. She winched." Belle "winched" like a startled porpoise. "That's when I drug the story out of her. She says, 'He struck me, the brute.'"

"Did she specifically mention her husband?"

Belle swiveled her head in honest bewilderment, her voice indignant. "If her husband don't beat her, who would?" Belle squatted again, resuming her re-enactment. "Then she pulls up her sleeve. . . ." Belle thrust up her own sleeve almost to the shoulder, gazed in astonishment at mottled bruises on her arm and said indignantly, "Why, the so-and-so! Now how'm I gonna do a strip . . ." She suddenly recalled her audience and whipped down her sleeve, finishing triumphantly, "And I seen the bruises."

Fentress shot a quick, inquiring look at the doctor, who nodded once. Felix was on his feet by Fentress' desk, trying to make himself heard as Dick thrust himself past the woman and faced Fentress.

"Are you going to let this cheap, tenth-rate burlesque queen get away with those lies? It's just sensationalism, probably to promote that cheap, rotten dive in which she . . ."

The redhead darted out and whirled Dick around. "Listen, you smug hunk of nothing, just because a girl works in a night club, doesn't mean she's lying."

Dick backed off from the kitten-size girl with the tiger-size fury, his eyes cold. "And who's paying you to back up this . . ."

She slapped him. "I don't buy easy, shyster."

Dick fingered his jaw. "I'm not a lawyer," he said defensively, as if that were the only part of her statement he'd heard.

"Then don't make like one, Buster. Sadie's telling this story." The redhead stood belligerently waiting. Sadie, however, was not telling any story. She was watching her militant defense, her heavy face slack with astonishment. Under the redhead's sharpening gaze she shivered involuntarily and gulped. . . .

"Bruises," she repeated. At another firm nod she added. "I seen 'em . . ."

Dick backed cautiously away from the redhead and turned to Fentress. "I can prove she's lying. To the hilt." He glanced back at the redhead. "I can." In those two words Bill sensed a bellicose apology.

The redhead lowered her chin, her hands working, like a kitten sharpening its claws. "Harvard!" she accused him with all the malevolence of a Yale man.

"Groton, too." At Dick's accompanying grin the redhead stiffened, cocking her head to peer up at him appraisingly. Her hands stopped working. "And in spite of those handicaps, I can prove she's lying." Dick was once more assured and casual, and the redhead seemed momentarily uncertain, her guard still up.

"Suppose you do that, Mister Barnes," Fentress suggested mildly.

Dick pulled his eyes away from the redhead. "Huh? Oh, sure." He barely nodded to Belle. "She said it was Friday that Penny was so badly bruised that she winced just sitting down." Fentress accepted that and Dick went on,

"But on Saturday morning, the next day, I played tennis with Penny—in a halter and shorts."

"I bet you looked cute in 'em," the redhead murmured.

Dick flushed. "Penny wore 'em, and she played a fast if erratic game of tennis—without wincing. And there were no bruises!"

Bill shut his eyes, remembering. Penny in red halter and blue shorts, her skin gloriously tan, warm and exciting and unblemished.

Belle licked her lips. "She coulda used pancake. I do."

"That's a kind of make-up," the redhead explained with sweet formality. "As an ex-showgirl, Penny would know about it. It covers bruises."

Dick snorted. "Does it also cover wincing? Tennis is a strenuous game, using the muscles of the forearm particularly."

"And a racket and a little white ball that bounces." The redhead jutted her chin belligerently. "Even the lower classes play tennis these days, Mister Barnes."

"Miss Kane! Mister Barnes!" Fentress protested wearily. "Could you settle this class feud somewhere else? Right now I'd like a little supporting evidence. Miss Forbes, did anyone besides you see these bruises?"

Belle opened her mouth and left it open as she shook her head.

"They're not something a woman would brag about," the redhead pointed out.

Fentress ignored that and turned to Dick. "Can anyone confirm your story of the Saturday tennis game?"

"Bill, of course. And Janet."

Felix said smoothly, "He'd want more disinterested witnesses."

"I saw it." Miss Emily shook herself out of her spectator role. "No bruises. And no make-up I could see. But now I guess you'll say I wasn't a disinterested witness."

Felix urged Dick with, "There must have been others around the club who saw you playing."

"I could give you their names," Dick offered. "Some of 'em."

"The country club set," the redhead disparaged.

"I'd like their names in your formal statement, if you don't mind," Fentress suggested in a tone that dared anyone to refuse. "You'll all make one, I'm sure."

Casey herded them out of the room, Belle a little crestfallen now that her moment in the limelight was over, Miss Emily curiously subdued and thoughtful, Dick bending to speak to the redhead who ignored him pointedly. Felix, his briefcase sheathed under his arm like an unused weapon, waited at the desk. Bill walked over to Fentress. "Are you planning to hold me?"

The investigator flapped his hands. "After that? Just don't leave town suddenly."

Bill followed the others into the corridor, puzzling over the contradictions he had heard, making no sense out of them. Miss Emily clutched Belle Forbe's fat arm and leaned close to the blondined hair.

"Dearie, where do you get your girdles?"

Chapter VIII

After depositions had been made, with duly noted objections from Felix, Bill sat back in the ancient Packard, listening to Miss Emily. "But, Bill, nothing cements friendship between fat girls like a little swap on girdle information. And we need to be friends with her."

"Why? She was lying."

"You mean that you didn't beat Penny? Might have been good if you had. Not that. I knew she was lying about the hat."

"Hat?" He felt he'd lost part of the conversation. "She never mentioned a hat."

"That's how I know she was lying." As Bill blinked Miss Emily sighed gustily. "Don't suppose you ever noticed Penny's hats."

Bill thought back. "Well, there was a green one. . . ." His hand described an ascending spiral over his head. "It wound up."

"Bill, your wife wore the gawd-damnedest hats anybody ever saw. No woman who ever saw one could resist describing it. *She* didn't, so she was lying." Miss Emily bellowed instructions to Bailey to do several things simultaneously that were not only illegal but impossible, and came back to her argument. "So somebody put her up to that story.

And we're going to find out who that somebody is. Maybe
we'll find the killer."

Miss Emily had declared herself in on the investigation.

Bill felt a wild impulse to lean out a window and shout
a warning to innocent bystanders. He had seen Miss Emily
in action. Instead he sat back, marveling that he could
even think humorously.

Miss Emily's big freckled hand clamped down on his
knee. "Somebody's lying. Have to be. Take 'em one by one.
. . ." She was ticking off points on her fat, many-ringed
fingers. "The appointment call. You say it was made. Dick
denies it. You both could be right. Somebody else made
it—the murderer. And the missing memo . . ." Miss Emily
stuck up a stumpy thumb. "Why missing?"

They went over that looking for possibilities. Perhaps,
in that unaccountable burst of cleaning, Penny had thrown
it away. But surely the police would have found it.

"The murderer took it," Miss Emily stated with finality.
"Bill, it's going to be that way. Makes it simpler, too."

"Simpler? How?"

"Bill Taylor!" She rapped his knees sharply with her
stick. "You're not thinking!" Her voice softened hastily.
"Of course you're not. But you've got to. You're in a jam."

"I know I am. But how does the murderer's taking the
memo make it any simpler?"

Miss Emily shook herself deeper into the seat and
rubbed the knob of her stick thoughtfully. "If he swiped
the memo, it means he made the call. If he made the call,
he had to know about your deal with Bedford."

"Only four of us knew about that. Me, Penny, Dick and
Janet."

"Six," stated Miss Emily firmly. "Bedford knew about
it." She hesitated and then went on. "And I knew." She
waited. Bill couldn't think of a thing to say, and finally

she resumed, "Tony Bedford talked it over with me. The old rapscallion wanted to know if you are dependable."

"Am I?"

"Aside from robbing my orchard at the age of twelve and shooting my prize peacock . . ."

"I thought it was a wild turkey," Bill explained as earnestly as he had once sixteen years earlier.

Miss Emily snorted. "Green turkeys!" She shook herself. "Aside from those little things I told him you were fairly reliable. He wanted to know if you had enough initial capital."

Bill nodded. "For heavy-duty equipment. That's worried me. With my credit rating and a dime I can ride a streetcar."

"I told him you had it."

"Where would I get thirty thousand dollars?"

"From your Uncle Ralph." Miss Emily peered at him quizzically.

"I don't borrow from Uncle Ralph. Maybe that's why we're still friends as well as relatives. But thanks for the boost to Bedford."

"You could borrow against your inheritance." Miss Emily urged it with a curious insistence.

"That's pretty nebulous collateral. Uncle Ralph's still a fairly young man—and healthy. And anyway, he could change his will tomorrow." He shrugged. "Or he could have done it yesterday."

"Oh, you knew about his will?"

"He told me, when Penny and I were married. But, good Lord, Miss Emily, I've never even thought about Uncle Ralph's money. Anyway, he ought to spend it having his own good time, which he seems to be doing."

Miss Emily sank back with a gusty sigh. "All right. I told Tony you were getting the money from me."

"Oh!" It made him feel warm and comfortable to know Miss Emily had that much trust in him, and at the same time it embarrassed him to try to express his thanks.

"Don't try," she went on as if she had read his thoughts. "It's strictly business. I'll want a chattel mortgage on the equipment at six percent and a slice of the net. A big slice. I'm not very charitable."

Bill could feel himself grinning.

"Anyway, that's not the point." Miss Emily rattled her beads. "Six of us knew about it. Did anybody else?"

"Oh, we talked it over with Felix, naturally. He's our lawyer, and as close as a mandamus to a writ. And Dick and Janet wouldn't mention it."

Miss Emily waited a long moment that grew increasingly uncomfortable. "And Penny?"

A few hours ago Bill could have answered that questioning tone firmly, but now . . . "I don't see why she'd have told anyone."

"You didn't know she'd talked to that Forbes hag."

"No." And he was only beginning to realize how appallingly little he did know about Penny, except that he had loved her.

Miss Emily didn't press the point. She went back to fundamentals. "So six—no, seven people knew about the deal. Any one of them could've told a dozen others. Spreads the possibilities around for the police to consider. Keeps it narrow enough for us to check. At least you're not locked up and you're walking around more or less free."

"More or less?"

Miss Emily jerked her thumb eloquently over her shoulder. "A very inconspicuous coupé picked us up at the court house and has followed us very inconspicuously ever since. And don't turn your head around like an owl. Use that rear-view mirror. I had it put in especially so I could look out for speed cops." Miss Emily sighed gustily. "They're the only men who chase me these days."

Bill felt suddenly self-conscious. In the mirror he could see the coupé. "Are you sure that's a cop?"

"You're being tailed," Miss Emily stated with grim relish, and hunched forward in her seat, bellowing at Bailey, "Lose that car!"

Chapter IX

As Bill thrust open the door he heard movement in the kitchen, the light, clattering "tink" of metal on metal, followed by the hollow "chonk" of a closing door. The refrigerator door! Penny was here! Penny was back, miraculously restored! No, not restored. She'd never been gone. He'd dreamed it all. He'd drowsed off in the warm sunshine at the Bedford farm and dreamed this unholy day! He started for the kitchen door.

It opened to an oblong of light and she stood there, silhouetted against the glaring whiteness of the kitchen, a slim, gay figure waving a small saucepan.

"Penny!" He stumbled in his eagerness to reach her.

The saucepan drooped, the slim figure in the doorway sagged momentarily, then straightened. "Bill, I thought you'd need something to eat after . . ." He knew that light, breathy catch of voice.

Of course it wasn't Penny, and the dream was a monstrous reality. He stopped, bracing against the overlarge table that crowded the narrow hall. Very carefully he placed his hat on the table.

"Hello, Janet."

She took three running steps and laid her hand on his arm, her face tilted up. Her mouth, a little too large for beauty, worked before words came. Finally she said with that catchy breathlessness of hers, "I can't tell you how grieved I am for you."

"Thanks, Janet." He dropped one arm across her shoulders and squeezed lightly. "You're a pal." He eyed the pan. "I'm not hungry." Not hungry, just vastly empty; hollow inside, with a shell outside that looked and moved and spoke like Bill Taylor.

"Coffee, then." She tugged, and he held back mulishly. "You can always use coffee," she urged. He was surprised at the strength in her slender arms and slim brown hands.

Smells hit him, coffee overreaching the rich, spicy fragrance of cinnamon and baking bread, and with the smells came weakness, a quivery weakness back of the knees and deep inside, so that he was grateful for the stool Janet expertly hooked behind him.

She turned away, reaching into a cabinet for cups, stretching on tiptoe, the dark seams of her stockings straight and taut, her slim hips pushed against the light summery skirt. Janet was slender, yes, but how could he have mistaken that firm, trim figure for Penny's honed-down perfection? Janet was taller, too. The differences should have been apparent at once, the moment she opened the kitchen door. It was just that he had wanted to see Penny, had geared his mind and his eyes for her. Was that what had happened to Penny out there by the telephone? Had she been expecting him back and, seeing a silhouetted figure there, automatically taken it for Bill, regardless of size or shape? He started up before he remembered the phone call didn't matter that way. It was false. Someone had pretended to be Penny, pretended to see, to scream— in order to put a rope around Bill's neck.

Janet's voice recalled him, saying, "Drink this." He accepted the cup absently and drank.

"Yow!" He spluttered hot coffee on the linoleum. "Wow, that's hot!" He hadn't expected that, probably because Penny's coffee usually had reached him lukewarm.

"Nibble on that till I have eggs and bacon ready." Janet thrust a warm, buttery cinnamon bun into his free hand. "This is just a pick-up meal, Bill. We can eat right here in the kitchen."

He nodded, leaning his shoulders against the wall, stretching out his long legs, virtually subdividing the kitchen. Janet had to hop over his legs every time she made one of her quick sparrow trips to the pantry, turning to ask, "Where do you keep the pepper? Where's the butter dish? Got any hickory-smoked salt? I'm looking for the chives."

Between munches on the bun he'd point vaguely and not too hopefully at the pantry, or the spice shelf or the windowsill. Finally, in a crescendo of clatter, Janet told him to sit at the table and he sat obediently, snatching another bun, which Janet promptly took away from him. "Get some nourishment in you, first."

The fluffy yellow eggs, flecked with hickory-smoke salt and delicately spiked with chopped chives, were nourishment that he realized he needed only after he began to feel less empty and quivery. He held out his cup for another refill of coffee.

"That's four," Janet cautioned. "You won't sleep a wink."

"Never bothers me," he stated loftily. "I sleep like a . . ."

They both held it, remembering he had something else that would keep him awake tonight. Janet suddenly busied herself with a pan of buns. Bill took one and then set it aside deliberately.

"Look, Janet," he leaned his elbows on the table and rested his chin on balled fists, "I can't hide from it. And my friends can't edit their conversations so as not to remind me of it. It's done, and so we might as well bring it out in the open. My wife has been murdered." He stopped, choked.

"Don't, Bill." Janet's voice was a small whimper of protest.

He had control again. "I'm shocked, bewildered. After that first moment, I haven't felt grief. I can't feel it yet. Probably because I'm numb. I guess I'm like a man whose leg has just been amputated. They say he has the illusion that it's still there, even when he can see it's gone. It's like that with me. I can't help but think that Penny is just out somewhere and will be coming in any minute, full of the things that happened today, people she saw on streetcars. . . ." He was talking easily about Penny again. "I was so glad she was beginning to go out with your crowd. She didn't seem to get along with 'em at first, but last week . . ." He laughed. "Why, this past week she was just like a hometown matron. Four luncheons with 'the girls.'" He held up one finger. "Tuesday, Ella Fields. Wednesday . . ."

"How's Ella's baby?" Janet looked hurt. "She hasn't let me see it."

Bill scowled, thinking back. "Penny didn't mention a baby. On Wednesday she took Fay Compton to the Mirror Room for tea."

"Bill . . ." Janet was frowning at him perplexedly.

"And Friday she had lunch with Marge . . ." He snapped his fingers. "I never can remember her married name. Satterthwaite! That it?"

"Bill, did you tell this to the police?" Something in her expression killed his enthusiasm.

"Ella just had a baby last week and they're not letting her see anyone. She nearly died. Fay is in the hospital for an appendectomy, and Marge Satterthwaite left two weeks ago to join her husband on the West Coast." Janet spent a long moment over her final sip of coffee. Finally she set the cup down. "It's better to hear it from me than from the police. And if you tell them, instead of letting them investigate and find out."

Bill stupidly regarded the bun he was holding, letting her words soak in. Penny hadn't had those luncheon dates. He finally got words out. "Just tell them my wife lied to me? They already know that—or else I lied to them. Either way seems to suit Fentress." He spoke bitterly, knowing it wasn't quite the truth. "All he wants is discrepancies. Well, he's getting them."

"Don't be bitter. It isn't like you. And you won't be saying your wife told you lies. You'll be pointing out specific clues to them. If Penny wasn't with Marge or Ella or Fay, who was she with? If the police can find that out . . ."

"They won't need to. Fentress will say, 'Another man,' and that'll be my motive for killing her. The worst of it is, it could be like that. Another man, I mean."

"Bill!" Janet set her cup down firmly. "You can't say things like that about Penny." Under his surprised gaze she shrugged. "All right. I didn't like Penny, so it seems odd I'm defending her. And to you, of all people. But don't you realize that if the police think you doubted Penny, they'll have their motive strengthened? So you can't afford even to think things like that. So I'm not defending Penny so much as protecting you. And you could be wrong."

It surprised Bill how meekly he took Janet's firm little lecture. Her last point astonished him. "Wrong? How?"

"She may have been forced to lie. About the lunch dates, I mean. To protect you."

"Protect me?" Incredulity sent his voice high, and he brought it down. "What would I need protecting from?"

Janet scowled into her cup, turning it studiedly. "I'm not sure I can explain it, Bill, but we know Penny was in trouble—trouble that caught up with her and killed her.

Not just 'trouble' but some specific person who meant
trouble. Most likely a man." Janet swirled the cup slightly.
"I'm not telling this well—but suppose she was stalling
this person, this man, who might come to you. Possibly
with some story about Penny's past. Either true or not."

"I'd've killed him!"

"Exactly. So Penny tried to keep him away from you,
only she tried too long." She threw up her hands. "Something like that."

He smiled across the table at her. "Thanks for a nice
try. And it could be like that. I'll tell Fentress in the
morning." Weariness was overcoming him, and there were
so many things to be done. He thought of one with a start.
"I've got to call Uncle Ralph."

"I'll take care of the other arrangements. That's mainly
what I came for."

The "other arrangements" meant the funeral, flowers,
notifying the right people, all the mundane accompani-
ments of death. "Thanks. You're a wonderful help." He
stood by her chair, hand on her shoulder.

Janet grinned up at him. "The perfect secretary, that's
me."

He left her straightening the kitchen and dialed long
distance. In a surprisingly short time he heard Donny's
rich baritone. "Who this?"

"Donny, I want to speak to Uncle Ralph." He heard
Donny's long-drawn gasp. "Donny! Donny! This is Bill.
Bill Taylor. I want to speak to . . ."

"I heard you, Mistuh Bill. I heard you. How-come you
didn't git here? We waited for you. Helt up the funeral two
days. . . ."

"Funeral? Donny! Whose? Is Uncle Ralph there?"

"He was kilt last Wednesday. Tryin' out one o' them
new foreign cars. I tole him lemme test it, but he—" Donny's warm, deep voice broke—"he went hisself."

Bill felt the muscles of his face tighten. Not Uncle
Ralph! He enjoyed living too much. For him just sheer
living had been fun. And now he was dead.

Donny's voice caught and went on. "We got the wire,
Mistuh Bill, sayin' you was out of town, but we was hopin'
you'd git back in time."

"I haven't been . . . What wire?"

"Mistuh Dick's wire. Your partner." Donny seemed to
have full control now. "The funeral was yestiddy, Mistuh
Bill, and Mistuh Cake, that's the lawyer, he's on the way
to see you."

Bill exchanged a few more helpless, broken sentences
with the old man before he hung up. He was still staring
at the phone when Janet brushed by him on the way to the
front door.

Miss Emily hurtled in, her stick thudding. "Of all the
confounded stupid stunts!" She thumped her stick impe-
riously. "Either get that woman out of here or I stay as
chaperone."

"Huh?" Bill swiveled out of the chair and stood up.
"What woman? Out of where?"

"Her!" For an instant Bill was afraid Miss Emily was
going to brain Janet with her stick, but she stopped an
inch short of destruction.

"That's Janet," he said stupidly.

"I've got eyes. I know it's Janet."

"We don't need a chaperone." Janet held herself stiffly.

"Only people I know who don't, then," Miss Emily
snapped, and leaned on her stick, scowling first at Janet
and then Bill. "Only I don't mean it that way. Haven't you
two got a grain of sense? As soon as my back is turned . . ."

"Just what is all this about, Miss Emily?" Janet made
it firm.

"The police. You should have thought of it, Janet, if
Bill didn't. He isn't capable of thinking, right now. They

only need a little more motive and—bing!" Miss Emily rapped the banister sharply. "He's behind bars."

"And what's this motive?" Bill made his voice cold and flat.

"The 'other woman.' Janet. The girl you once jilted."

"I jilted Janet?"

"Miss Emily, really, this is absurd." Janet colored.

"Is it? Not to the police, if they knew you were alone here with Bill," Miss Emily sniffed the air like a hungry mastiff, "cooking his meals."

"I'd do as much for a dog, Miss Emily."

"Bill doesn't happen to be a dog. He's a man. A very personable man—and very recently a widower—and heir to five million dollars."

Bill started a protest, saw her point and shut his mouth. He'd have to protect Janet, too. Then Miss Emily's last remark caught up with him. "How do you know I'm heir to five million dollars? Uncle Ralph . . ."

" . . . has been dead since last Wednesday. You forget, Bill, that I own the newspapers in this town, and I read 'em, even if nobody else does." She glared around at them, her eyes narrowing. "Or *did* somebody read it?" Her sharp blue eyes closed thoughtfully and then opened very wide. One big, freckled hand clutched at her medallion. She gasped. "Water! Get me some water! I feel faint."

Bill was already drawing water in the kitchen before he realized that Miss Emily had the constitution of an ox and had never felt faint in her life.

Chapter X

When Bill returned with the glass of water Miss Emily was hunched into a chair, her hands and chin propped on the knob of her stick. She was glaring at Janet. Janet, he noted with some surprise, was glaring right back. Janet had never seemed the sort of person who could glare, and Miss Emily was definitely not the person to practice on. However, Janet seemed to be holding her own, though her cheeks were flushed and her hair was softly rumpled, as if she had run her fingers distractedly through it.

Miss Emily's sharp, ice-blue eyes flickered to his face and back to Janet. "You should get mad more often."

"I'm not mad," Janet stated furiously. "I'm flabbergasted."

"Stay flabbergasted. On you it looks good." Miss Emily shifted her eyes back to Bill. "And what in tarnation are you bringing me water for?"

"You felt faint." Bill extended the glass, feeling awkward and about eight years old.

"Never felt faint in my life. And if I did, I'd revive enough to sock the guy that brought me water. Haven't you any whiskey?" As he turned to go she yelled after him, "Good whiskey. None of those fancy-pants drinks. Sipping stuff! All taste and no swallow." Her voice grumbled off into minor complaints about the general poor quality of

whiskey these days, while Bill bent and fumbled among the
bottles of Pernod, curacao, creme de menthe, anisette and
cointreau with which Penny had stocked their small bar.
She had preferred the exotic drinks Miss Emily scorned.
He paused, his hand on his own private bottle of bourbon. Scotch! Penny had drunk her last drink in Scotch,
poisoned Scotch. He stooped lower and peered among the
oddly shaped bottles. No Scotch. He couldn't recall getting any, either. Not recently. Then the murderer must have
brought his own bottle, drugged. Bill shivered. That made
Penny's murder seem more horribly cold-blooded than ever,
mercilessly premeditated, ruthlessly done. He must remember to tell Fentress about the Scotch, or lack of it. He
straightened, shaking off his shivers. "I've got bourbon."

"Be generous, Bill. I'm tired."

He was, by normal standards, over-generous. She eyed
the tumbler gratefully and swallowed with an enthusiasm
that made his own throat ache.

"Ah! I needed that." She handed back the glass. "And
offer Janet a drink," she commanded.

Belatedly he turned to Janet but she shook her head,
her eyes still angry. Miss Emily, he realized, could rile an
angel. She went on to do her best. "You're both fools, of
course. The police are going to suspect any woman you
jilted . . ."

"Miss Emily!" Janet leapt from her chair, her cheeks
flaming.

"Oh, sit down, Janet! You're not the only person who
found Bill attractive—with or without five million dollars."

"That's absurd." Bill fumbled around trying to say just
how absurd. "Look. I never jilted Janet. There never was
anything like that. Good Lord, Miss Emily, we've been
friends for years, since she was a kid. It never occurred to
me . . ."

"It occurred to Janet."

Bill looked unhappily at Janet for denial and, though she was shaking her head stubbornly, he knew there was at least a modicum of truth in what Miss Emily said.

He rumpled the wiry brush of his hair distractedly, then turned to Miss Emily. "Look, just suppose there was some girl who—well, wanted me for a rich husband. She's ruined her chance of getting me if I'm convicted of Penny's murder."

"Yes." Miss Emily watched him shrewdly.

"Then certainly this woman you dreamed up wouldn't commit a murder and then frame *me* for it."

"There's jealousy," Miss Emily produced, but without conviction.

"In that case the money doesn't enter into it." Bill was a little surprised that he could think so logically at a time like this. "And anyway, was that in the paper? That Uncle Ralph had left me his money?"

"No," Miss Emily admitted. "Just an account of the accident. Ralph was a national sports figure, you know. And that ass of a city editor missed the boat, too. No local tie-in. No mention of you. Just stuck the item back on page eleven."

"I didn't even see that item, but then, Penny usually had the paper so scattered by the time I came home . . ." He broke off. "If it wasn't in the paper, how did you know about it?"

Miss Emily cocked a surprised eye at him. "I witnessed Ralph's will." She screwed down one eyebrow and peered at him. "Are you getting at what I think you're getting at?"

For an instant Bill felt bafflement. He hadn't carried the idea any further. Now, slowly, he did and the result surprised him. "If it wasn't in the paper, how would anyone know about my inheritance?"

Miss Emily sighed. "You got it, too. And I don't know the answer. But somebody did know."

"You knew. . . . But after learning of Uncle Ralph's death you didn't publicize the inheritance. Else Penny would have seen it. And nothing could have kept her from yelling to the housetops about five million dollars."

Miss Emily nodded. "That's just it, Bill. She did know." She held up one big hand to stem Bill's protest. "Or I thought she did. You see, that's the excuse Penny gave me on the phone for the surprise party—to celebrate your new millions."

"But that wasn't Penny on the phone. The police proved she couldn't have made that call. But even so, why didn't you tell me?"

"Damn it, Bill, there wasn't any point in telling you something I assumed you knew. If Penny knew, you certainly would. Then when I learned the phone call was faked, I assumed the story of Ralph's death and your inheritance was false, too. Especially since you hadn't heard of it. It wasn't until I checked the paper, a few minutes ago, that I knew it was true. Then I realized how important that phone call about the inheritance really was."

"How important is it, really?" Janet spraddled her legs, set an elbow on each knee and planted her firm little chin on knotted fists.

Miss Emily squinted fiercely up at Bill as if daring him to deny what she was about to say. "Money like that—millions—is an invitation to blackmail. If you're in a position to be blackmailed. And a girl like Penny—well, she could be in a spot."

Bill was grateful she hadn't said anything about the baby to Janet. He picked up her argument hastily. "And the blackmailer could have quarreled with her when she refused to knuckle under."

Miss Emily nodded and Bill breathed easier. That took the pressure off his friends and put it on some unknown hiding behind the anonymous mask of a blackmailer.

Miss Emily went on nodding like a porcelain mandarin, mechanically and evenly. "But still it has to be some one who knew about the Bedford deal."

With that sentence Miss Emily had placed it squarely back among his friends. "And it had to be somebody close enough to all of us to realize, when they saw that item, that you'd inherit his money."

"I never would have thought of it myself."

Miss Emily stirred in her seat. "Incidentally, Bill, what happens to your money?"

"I spend it."

"I mean when you die."

"You mean my will? I felt silly making a will, but Felix said I should. For the partnership. So Dick and I made reciprocal wills, leaving the business to the survivor, so it wouldn't be broken up just to satisfy some heirs."

"So the way it stands, Dick gets everything if you die?"

"Well, after Penny and I were married Felix fixed up a codicil so that Penny would get all my real property and a life interest in the business. That way, my death wouldn't break up the business and she'd get her share as long as she lived."

"She didn't live very long," Miss Emily muttered.

"No." Bill was able to say it without bitterness; it was simply a fact.

"So the codicil is out." Miss Emily nodded her own answer, before Bill could speak.

"I suppose so."

"And Dick gets everything."

"Wait a minute! At the time those wills were drawn up neither of us had anything, except the business." Bill shoved his hands deep in his pockets, jingling his keys angrily. "And that wasn't much. It still isn't.

"But now you've got five million dollars and Dick has half-interest in a business that isn't much. With Penny dead and you convicted, he gets a half-interest or more in five million dollars."

"That's crazy. Dick didn't even know about Uncle Ralph." Bill felt his voice dying. Dick had known. Donny had just said Dick had wired him. But Dick never told me. He never once mentioned knowing Uncle Ralph was dead, even though he's known since last Thursday.

Chapter XI

Bill went to phone Fentress, since he had to tell him about the inheritance. Fentress, however, wasn't available, until Miss Emily took the phone away from Bill and bullied the desk sergeant into locating him. Located, the investigator was not happy with Miss Emily's report about her knowledge of Bill's inheritance.

"Charles, I started to tell you, but you jumped down my throat. I don't like people who jump down my throat. And anyway, you were so darned earnest about proving the call was a fake I thought sure the story of Ralph's death was a fake, too. . . . Not another deposition! Oh, all right. And you'll want to talk to Bill." She thrust the phone into his hand, snorting.

Bill managed to convince him, or seemed to, that he had only learned of his inheritance within the hour. He reported the telegram, which baffled them both, it seemed so pointless, and brought up the matter of the Scotch, which Fentress seemed to accept.

"And now, Taylor, I've got some information for you. We were lucky. A quick check in Washington on your wife's fingerprints got us a lead. She worked in a war plant in Jersey in '45, and from them we got her address and traced her father." He sighed slightly. "I can't say I blame her for changing her name. She used to be Maggie Hutzler. And

her father, Gus, is a janitor. He'd like to come on here for
formal identification and for the funeral, but claims he's
broke. Now the department . . ."

"I'll send him a check. Will five hundred do?"

"Ample. But after all, you're a millionaire now." Fentress sighed dreamily.

"Speaking of that, I may have to go to Cincinnati.
Uncle Ralph's affairs . . ."

"Actually, Bill, I haven't the authority to stop you and
therefore not the authority to tell you you can go. However, if you'd tried to leave without letting me know, I'd
soon have gotten the authority." He said it amicably, but
under the lightness Bill recognized an implacable stern-
ness. "Tell you what. Call in Jim Brady. He's the big fellow
outside. At least he should be there. If you're willing to
take him along, at your own expense, of course . . ."

"Glad to. And thanks." Bill hung up and sat staring
at the phone. So Penny had lied about her origin? Well,
with a janitor for a father he didn't much blame her. And
the name! In show business it would have been deadly. He
shook himself and went to the door.

The man who answered his call was astonishingly big,
with a wide, easy grin. "Brady's the name. Jim Brady. The
boss figured they'd need somebody big if you tried to make
a break." He measured Bill's size against his own cheerful-
ly. "It'd take somebody big to handle you." He offered his
credentials to Bill, who merely glanced at them, but Miss
Emily took them for suspicious scrutiny.

"It says here you're F. M. Brady. That doesn't come out
'Jim.'" She glared at him, head lowered.

Brady sighed, as if this were a customary inquisition.
"My mother was romantic. She read Scott's novels, Can
you figure what would happen to a cop that went around
calling himself Fitzjames Marmaduke?"

Miss Emily handed the card back, twinkling. "Anyway, you look something like Diamond Jim. He used to visit our house. He was bigger than you, though. Heavier."

"Food was cheaper then," Brady reclaimed his credentials and looked at Bill. "What's up?"

Bill explained the possibility of a trip, and Brady nodded. "I'll check in with the boss, and we can leave any time." He reached for the phone.

"And, Brady, since you have to be around, you might as well stay here," Bill offered, and Brady looked briefly surprised at the invitation.

"Thanks." He grinned his acceptance and picked up the phone.

While he was talking the doorbell rang, and Bill answered it, holding out his hand. "Mister Cake!" He had a long-time affection for his uncle's attorney, friend and ardent admirer, who looked as plump, frosted and freshly baked as his name.

"Delighted to see you, Bill, except for the doubly tragic circumstances." He bounced jovially into the hall, greeted Miss Emily with affection, was introduced to Janet and Brady, still on the phone, and settled himself plumply in a chair, a briefcase as plump and sleek as himself at his surprisingly small feet. "Understand perfectly why you couldn't attend the funeral. Tragic thing, your wife's death. Just heard of it. I drove down, you know. In one of Ralph's cars. The MG. It's yours now. Miss Emily, you're looking fit as a fiddle."

Miss Emily snorted. "Bass fiddle. And about the same shape. Did they give Ralph a good send-off?

"Stuffy. Terribly stuffy. Very solemn affair." Mister Cake bobbed out of the chair to look appropriately solemn. "Six state senators for pallbearers. That sort of thing. Too many flowers, of course. Ralph would have preferred a calliope." The round little man bounced on his toes, as if that might add the illusion of height to his roundness. Instead it merely emphasized his resemblance to a very new tennis ball. "However, he was aware it wasn't appropriate, so he didn't request it. On account of the Board of Directors, you know." He addressed that to Bill. "Or if you don't, you'll have ample time to find out. They run the company as if they were saying High Mass. Or you can take over, if you care to. You're the majority stockholder, you know. Oh, botheration!" Mister Cake clucked. "I shouldn't have said that until after the will's read, but you knew it, of course."

"I never thought much about it. It seemed pretty remote." Bill let himself be placed in a large, comfortable chair while Mister Cake shoved the near-modern coffee table into a position of his liking. "Uncle Ralph looked like he was good for years."

"Oh, he was. He was. Or should have been. Except for a minor kidney complaint he was in prime condition. Prime." Mister Cake bounced himself behind the coffee table and peered over it for a final word with Bill. "Couldn't have raced those cars if he hadn't been." He sighed wistfully. "Must have been glorious. He was doing a hundred and thirty when he went over. Quick. Final."

Brady strolled into the room and Mister Cake looked up at him, nodded him to a chair and plunged his hand into his plump briefcase, producing a thin document. He began reading without glasses. Somehow Bill had expected him to wear glasses.

Bill paid little attention, beyond recognizing that the will gave modest sums to a couple of distant cousins of Uncle Ralph's and left Donny a really substantial amount for his years of faithful service. "The rest of my estate, real and personal, I will, devise and bequeath, free and clear, to my nephew, William Carey Taylor."

Mister Cake folded the stiff paper carefully and harrumphed twice as if he didn't quite trust his voice. "A most succinct document. Couldn't have done better if I'd written it myself."

Together he and Bill went over necessary details, death duties, taxes, disposal of certain real estate, all the complex technicalities of settling a big estate, until Bill felt he couldn't take any more. By mutual agreement they set a later date for fuller discussion and sat back to relax.

"Donny told me you received a telegram saying I was out of town."

"Yes, yes. From your partner. Barnes? Right. Well, Bill, don't distress yourself. Those things happen. It isn't as if you could have been with him in his last moments. There weren't any."

"I'd like to see that telegram." Bill must have spoken more sharply than he intended, for Mister Cake jerked upright, his mouth snapping shut.

"Certainly." He bent over the briefcase, fingers stiffly awkward. "It was with the rest of the correspondence."

"It's not that I doubt your words, sir. It's just that I was at home all last week, so it seems strange that Dick should have sent any such wire." He accepted the telegram from a mollified Mister Cake, who studied the back of it with his birdlike glance as Bill read.

"It looks genuine," the lawyer commented, cocking his head.

Bill passed the telegram to Brady, who spread it on the table for them all to see. Janet craned her head around, took a glance and shrugged. Miss Emily stabbed at it with her finger. "Why was it sent? That's the important thing. Dick didn't send it, I'm sure. Anyone can send a telegram and sign it whatever they want."

Mister Cake regarded the telegram thoughtfully. "Were you in the midst of an important deal? Something that required you to . . ."

"Not that important. And anyway, we'd decided to let it rest. No, I'm sure nobody kept Uncle Ralph's death from me for that reason."

Brady scowled at the yellow paper. "If you'd known about your Uncle's death, you'd have been in Cincinnati—and had an alibi."

"Good gracious!" Mister Cake looked startled. "Does he need an alibi?"

"I could use one. The one I have is full of holes."

Miss Emily shoved the telegram away from her and rested her several chins on her fists. "Let's look for what it did do, not for what might have happened."

"Huh?" Bill stared down at the telegram. "What did it do?"

"It kept Penny here at home, where the killer could get at her." Miss Emily, looking amazed, sat back so suddenly her beads jangled. "I'm brighter than I thought."

With that remark the yellow telegram assumed new and terrifying importance.

Chapter XII

Bill and Brady went down to the Western Union the following day.

The rather over-tailored young man behind the desk was not at first inclined to be co-operative, not until Brady leaned heavy arms on the counter and asked in a voice that overrode the clatter of typewriters and the hysterical chatter of telegraphy, "You rather talk this over down at the police station?"

The young man's elegant back stiffened and his shoulders winced as if an over-ripe tomato had found a target. "Police?" He said it in a scared whisper, and then coughed his voice back to normal preciseness. "Why didn't you say this was a police matter?"

He hurried away to comply with Bill's request and Brady winked after him. "He doesn't have to do it without a court order, but he's got a nervous conscience."

The young man returned with a sheaf of flimsies.

Brady flipped through them, stopped at one and stared at it. "It was sent from here." He pointed to the pink duplicate and Bill studied its coded intricacy.

One thing stood out. Beside a space marked "Phone" he saw his office number. It had originated from his office phone. Brady had seen it too and pointed it out to the young man.

"Can you tell us who phoned that in?"

The young man considered the flimsy for a moment, his finger tracing across a coded line of symbols. "I can tell you who said he was sending it. Mister Barnes," he pointed to the signature, "had his secretary phone it in." He tittered. "At least she said she was his secretary."

"Keep that handy," Brady cautioned him. "The D.A. will want to see it." Brady caught Bill's arm and was leading him out before he could protest. It was crazy. Secretary!

Janet!

But it couldn't be Janet. She hadn't known anything about Uncle Ralph's death until he'd talked to Donny, just last night, when she was at his house fixing supper. When Brady said they'd have to take the telegram in to Fentress, dully he led the way to the MG. He followed Brady's directions automatically, still trying to adjust to this new development, so that he barely heard Brady's words. "Barnes' secretary, huh? She's your secretary, too, ain't she? You sweet on her?"

"Janet? Lord, no! She's just an old friend."

"Janet? That's her name, huh? Same girl that was out at the house fixing your supper, ain't it?" Brady began a tuneless drone, his head nodding. He hadn't needed an answer.

"Just pull in there." Brady indicated the Commissioner's private parking space. "He's a pedestrian these days. His son's home from college." He guided Bill toward a small, discreet door on the side of the courthouse. "We'll go up in the private elevator, like the Mayor's relatives and big-shot gamblers."

So they arrived at Fentress' office by a route new to Bill and entered through a small anteroom. Through the connecting door he could see Fentress first, holding a plastic ruler too tightly, flexing it with white-knuckled hands.

Bill knew he was angry because his voice, usually suave, had an edgy rasp. "But you were there last night, weren't you? The very night of the crime. Why?"

Bill heard her voice before Brady pushed the door open wide enough for him to see her.

Janet!

"I'm not accustomed to having my charitable impulses questioned, Charles. And I intensely dislike the idea of you spying on me." She was standing by his desk, her chin high, her purse clasped tight under her breasts, her eyes defying the man across the desk.

Fentress slapped the ruler on the desk top—a new one—with a sound like a pistol shot. "Confound it, Janet, this is not a personal matter. I don't like your being involved any more than you do. Maybe less, because I don't get any adolescent kick out of being involved in murder. It's simply my job."

"So now I'm an adolescent! And as for your job . . ."

Fentress sighed wearily. "Janet, I apologize. I retract the 'adolescent.'" He almost grinned, stifled it. "And if this weren't such a grim business, I'd substitute 'childish.' You are behaving childishly, you know. You're not helping me, and your attitude is not helping Bill Taylor."

"Oh!" Janet's defiance sagged a little. "I'll do what I can."

"Good!" Fentress tapped at his chin with the ruler. "Now maybe we'll get somewhere. Can you tell me this?" The ruler swooped down and touched a paper on his desk. "How did that get in Taylor's home?"

"Why, Charles, you can be nice when you try. And of course I'd like to help." Janet's voice was purring gentleness. Too purring, too gentle, as Bill well knew. In a moment would come searing acid. It came. "But unfortunately I can't tell you how 'that,'" she aimed her purse at the paper, "got anywhere until I know what 'that' is."

"Oh!" Fentress slumped, looking bleak and yet almost as if he ruefully enjoyed the joke on himself. "That's what I get for playing policeman with the woman I love."

He saw Bill and straightened, coming out of his chair in one long lithe motion and stepping away from his desk as if, for the moment he wanted to disassociate himself from the official position it signified. After one bleak glance from Bill back to Janet, he smiled. "I'm glad you heard my declaration of affection. I'd rather have told you some other way, but I'm in love with Janet and I've just asked her to marry me. For the ninth time," he added.

Janet glanced at Bill, caught her breath and then laughed. "And after he found incriminating evidence, too."

Not the telegram! Fentress couldn't know this quickly.

"Bill, it was my way of expressing confidence in Janet despite what might look incriminating." He lowered his head bullishly. "And I have every confidence in her honesty and integrity, but none in her gullibility."

Janet smiled sweetly. "He says the nicest things. I'm adolescent, I'm childish and now I'm gullible. Don't you think it's nice of him to want to marry me in spite of my faults?"

Fentress ignored her, his eyes challenging Bill. Finally he stepped behind the desk and picked up the paper, pretending to study it again.

It took almost that long for Bill to catch up with the significance of what he'd heard. Janet and Fentress!

Fentress shook the paper, commanding attention. "This letter turned up in the course of the investigation." He stared over it at Bill. "In your bedroom. When the papers were sorted, this was sent for my attention."

"Routine." Bill heard the hoarse dry croak and knew Casey had joined them.

"I shall read it. I'd like to have you identify it."

Bill nodded.

"I have learned, my darling, that sometimes swift death can be merciful, so please try to think of it that way. She must have died almost instantly, without pain, so try not to grieve. And of course, sweetheart, I still love you. And always will. Just as soon as all this horror is over, we'll be married, just as I promised. A big church wedding with six bridesmaids and six ushers. We'll get that big house facing the sea, just as we've dreamed of, because I'll be filthy rich then."

Fentress looked up, staring at Bill. "Recognize that?"

Bill shook his head but without certainty. He glanced at Janet for guidance, but she was propping her head in her hand, her face hidden.

"There is a postscript: 'I have already made arrangements with Ben Tuthill to put up a simple headstone.' Does that help?"

"Ben Tuthill used to be my lawyer," Bill offered.

Fentress slapped the paper on the desk with the flat of his hand. "That letter is addressed to Janet Hayden. It was found in your bedroom and the handwriting has been identified. It is signed: 'Your future husband, Bill Taylor.' Now do you recognize it?"

"I never wrote that letter." Bill was quietly positive.

Fentress drew a long breath of relief.

Janet looked up at Bill from under her cupped hand, twinkling with malicious mischief. "Oh, but, Bill, you did write it."

Fentress let out his breath in a woosh. "Janet! You fool!"

Chapter XIII

"So now I'm a fool! It's surprising how many of my idiosyncrasies you put up with, Charles Fentress. But Bill
did write that letter." Janet leaned forward and pointed a
gloved finger at the paper, making it doubly explicit, doubly damning. "Ten years ago." Janet finished and sat back
triumphantly. "So of course he doesn't remember it."

Fentress clutched the letter, scanning it hastily. "But
ten years ago you were a child. And he refers to 'her death,'
obviously his wife. And then again, the money he inherited. 'I'll be filthy rich.' It's right here." Fentress tapped
the paper unhappily with a stiff, uncompromising finger.

Bill shut his eyes, thinking back ten years. No, Janet
was wrong. Nine years. A foxhole in the Pacific and a
tearstained letter from a kid. He'd answered it with that
letter.

Janet was already explaining. "He was being very sweet
to a little girl who had lost her dog—a silly little schoolgirl with an adolescent crush on him, who needed affection and the assurance that adolescent dreams would come
true. That was the most wonderful letter I ever got. And a
very kind man took time out from his own misery and war
and heartache to write it."

She was exaggerating, of course. It was just that he had
known the kid needed something to cling to, to ease her

over the loss of her dog, a little blond cocker he'd given her.

Fentress turned the paper from side to side as if in that way he could find some proof of what she said. Casey came over to study it across his shoulder. He pointed. "But, Loot, he says he'll be filthy rich." He glared around at Bill.

Bill was remembering. "I'd saved twelve hundred dollars, and I anticipated my severance pay. That seemed filthy rich to me."

Casey clamped his lips shut but he nodded. Apparently he could understand that twelve hundred dollars would seem filthy rich.

Fentress worried at the letter. "But he says he'll marry you when he gets back. If you were only twelve . . ."

Jane sat up indignantly. "I was thirteen, and a very precocious thirteen." Suddenly she smiled at Bill and then at Fentress. "Charles, haven't you ever told a little girl with big adoring eyes, 'I'll wait till you grow up and we'll get married.' A big church wedding with all the trimmings? Haven't you?" While Fentress gave the matter frowning deliberation, she smiled at Casey. "Haven't you?"

Casey grinned for the first time Bill could remember. "Kids don't go much for me. But I know what you mean."

Brady was grinning over his own memory. "There was a kid on our block—she was twelve—threw rocks at the church when I got married. I was in uniform then. Kids go for uniforms."

Janet cocked her head and eyed him appraisingly. "You'd look nice in a uniform."

Brady chuckled. "She got over it. Grew up and married a salesman just this year."

Fentress glared around, his urbanity ruffled. "This is not a Lonely Hearts club." Brady and Casey smoothed out their faces to efficient blankness, and Fentress turned to

Janet. "You've proved your point, if it was necessary. I'm aware that girls get adolescent crushes and men encourage them out of mistaken gallantry—or vanity."

"Oh, bother, Charles! Why don't you look for that 'internal evidence' you're always talking about? It's there. Right in the letter."

Bill tried to remember the phrasing as Fentress had read it. It was damning, and Fentress had a right to his doubts.

"What internal evidence?" Fentress pushed the letter to one side as if it had developed germs but he continued to study it.

"The mighty police! Why, Ben Tuthill, of course. He's been dead seven or eight years."

"Oh!" Fentress leaned over the letter to review the phrase. "Naturally I'll have to check on your statement about Tuthill."

"Dead, all right," Casey volunteered and Fentress almost wrenched himself around in his chair to look at him. Casey explained, "Six-seven years ago. He was always around court." As Fentress continued to glare, Casey added thoughtfully, "Before your time, though."

Janet stood up, tightening her gloves in quick emphatic little tugs. "Is the inquisition over?"

"Yes! No! I mean it wasn't an inquisition!" Fentress appealed unhappily to Bill. "Was it?" He drew a deep breath, held it and faced Janet. "All I wanted to find out was how that letter got in Taylor's house. He wrote it, but it obviously had been mailed."

Janet worked one glove out to smooth perfection, admiring it. "Why didn't you just ask me?"

Fentress' hands clenched tensely at air, as if he knew the impulse to murder; then he relaxed. "I will." He was formally correct. "How did this letter get back to Bill Taylor's house?"

Janet continued to admire the glove for a moment. Then:

"I don't know."

Fentress groaned. "But haven't you any idea?"

"I'm probably being very nasty, Charles—and you, particularly, Bill, I want to realize that. It's only my opinion and I could be way off, but I'm sure I'm not. Penny took that letter."

"Penny?" Fentress and Bill exploded together.

"I told you I'd be feminine and cruel. Or is that tautological? Anyway, Penny, didn't like me, so she used to come to see me."

Fentress opened his mouth to question this piece of feminine logic and then closed it, sighing. Janet went on.

"She snooped. Among my things. When I went to fix coffee. Several times, after she left, I found things in my desk—my home desk—out of order. She snooped through my office desk, too, when I wasn't there, but I didn't mind that. It wasn't personal. Just business things."

"About the letter," Fentress reminded her gently.

"Oh, yes. The letter. I noticed it missing after one of her visits. Last Thursday, as a matter of fact. I'd stayed home from the office with a headache and she came by—to see how I was, she said. But I think it was to check up on Bill. You see, she'd been by the office and found we were both out. She let that slip. Oh, quite accidentally, of course, but I'm sure it was to let me know she was keeping an eye on Bill. I was laid up in bed, but she puttered around the living room. Straightening up, she said. But when she left, I checked. She'd snooped. And the letter was missing."

Fentress picked up a pencil, held it poised. "Where did you keep the letter?"

"Behind a picture. You know, in the back." She made a graphic little pocket with one hand and stuffed the other down into it. "A photograph in a leather frame on my desk."

"Whose?" Fentress asked, and then added, with anguish of a man deliberately biting down on a sore tooth, "Bill's, I suppose?"

Janet shook her head and smiled very sweetly. "I tore all of Bill's up the day he got married." She grinned at Brady. "I was a little too old to throw rocks at the church."

Bill shut his eyes and swallowed. The little fool! She was deliberately leading Fentress up the garden path, intentionally throwing him another suspect—herself—to draw his attention from Bill. He knew he'd have to break this thing now, somehow nullify its importance before Fentress had time to weave it into a case against Janet. There was something in the back of his mind that cleared the whole thing up. Something Janet had said. Wait! He had it. He leaned forward eagerly.

"Janet, were you out of the office all day Thursday?" Janet, ready to launch another barb at Fentress, glanced around, startled. "Are you planning to dock my wages?" She smiled ferociously at Fentress. "See what kind of boss I have."

"You said you had a headache," Bill persisted. "And you didn't go to the office."

Janet's impishness faded a trifle.

"Thursday?" She nodded. "Yes, it was Thursday. A whole working day."

"You could prove it?"

"I don't usually . . ." Janet began tartly, and hesitated. The impish grin came back. "As a matter of fact I think I could, if I had to. Miss Busby—I think she's awfully well named—buzzed in with soup, her remedy for anything short of cancer, and I'm not sure of her attitude on that."

"And she stayed? All day?"

"You've met Miss Busby. Can you get rid of her? She reads. With gestures."

"She was there all day?"

"It seemed like a week. No, she wasn't there all day, Penny sort of eased her out when she came in."

"What time was that?"

"Bill, I suppose you've got a good reason for all this?" Janet's glance of annoyance cleared in a brief smile. "Of course you have. Let's see. It was the third bowl of soup, so it must have been about one o'clock when Penny came. I didn't look at my watch, but I remember Penny saying she had a luncheon date at one-thirty and she had to hurry. Only she didn't. She lingered. And snooped."

Bill heaved such a sigh of relief that Janet looked startled. He turned belligerently on Fentress. "All right, you can see that damn telegram. Janet couldn't have sent it."

Chapter XIV

". . . And he's' downstairs now, making formal identification."

"Who?" Janet had just left, but Bill was still in a daze of relief about the telegram and wasn't paying attention to Fentress.

"Gus Hutzler." When that didn't awaken anything in Bill, Fentress said a little sharply, "Penny's father. You paid his way here. But frankly, he hasn't been much help. He knows nothing about her later than the job in Newark, and she wasn't living at home even then. So we've still got those blank years to fill in."

"Wasn't Cameron a help?"

"Nothing we didn't already know. She sang at *El Camino* when he was there, the last year of the war. And of course that week in Caswell, where you met her. In between—a blank."

"What about her agent, this Ken Folsom?"

"We got his address from that photograph on your mantle. It was one of her professional shots."

Bill hadn't even realized that those over-glamorized pictures were part of Penny's professional past. "Was Folsom any help?" He no longer felt self-conscious asking for information about his wife from other men.

"A little. We caught up with him the afternoon of the murder, at rehearsal, at The Rendezvous. He'd been there since ten that morning, which is why we missed him at his office."

So Folsom, whom Bill remembered only vaguely being pointed out by Penny, had an alibi.

Fentress made the point lightly and went on. "He filled in a few scattered dates, which we're checking. However, he claims she was only one of hundreds of clients—the hundreds being an exaggeration, I'm sure. But we'll keep plugging. Somewhere along the line we'll hit what we're looking for."

"Unless it's right here in this room." Casey's hoarse monotone rasped along his nerves, reminding Bill he was the detective's favorite candidate. Casey clinched it with, "The D.A.'s getting itchy."

"I'm still in charge, Casey," Fentress began irritably, and grinned at his subordinate. "Until the D.A. breaks out in a rash."

"Okay." Casey shrugged his indifference, and jerked his squarish head at the door. "Poppa's outside."

"Bring him in."

Bill turned to face the door as a wispy little man shuffled through, his glance turned uneasily on Casey's arm guiding him, as if he weren't quite sure this was the normal function of a policeman. When Casey abandoned him at the desk he looked relieved, smiling nervously at Fentress.

"Howjadew." The little man reached for his hat, realized he had left it somewhere and jerked his hand down. "It's her all right. It's my Maggie." He sniffled loudly and rubbed a knuckle under his nose. "She's growed a lot, but I knowed her. Even beat up like that."

"You're positive?"

Gus Hutzler looked hurt. "I know my own girl, don't I? Even if she has went and peroxided her hair, and a sin and a shame it is on me she done it. Vanity! When she was home there wasn't no such sinful doin's. Paintin' her face and primpin'! I wouldn'ta stood for it. I don't hold with lipstick and nylon stockings and nail polish and perfumes with names like 'Temptation' and 'My Sin' and such." Gus Hutzler thumped his chest with a knotted, grimy fist. "Sinful! Lustful! That's what it is." He sniffled audibly. "Symbols of the devil, I say, but her maw weren't so perkitckler. 'She's young. Let the girl have a good time,' she says." Gus glared around the room. "And look where it's led to—her down there in the morgue with her hair dyed like a hussy."

Gus saw some profound connection between peroxided hair and Penny lying in the morgue downstairs, but it wasn't clear to Bill. He could only think irrelevantly that, for a man who didn't hold with such things, Gus had a pretty comprehensive knowledge of them.

Gus snuffled again. "It's my Maggie all right."

So Penny was formally identified. Maggie Hutzler. Bill had an idea this identification would strip still another illusion from those with which he had surrounded Penny. They've taken another little bit from me, and I can't seem to care.

But Gus had said something that didn't quite ring true. Bill started thinking back.

Gus was shifting in front of Fentress' desk, repeating uneasily, "I'da knowed her anywhere. She's my little girl, see. In spite of that there blondined hair. Had right purty hair, wunst." He sniffled drearily.

That was it! Gus, after eight or ten or maybe more years, might be able to identify his daughter, but Bill knew Penny, and one thing he was sure of. He spoke quietly. "Penny didn't peroxide her hair. She used to brag she didn't need to."

Gus craned around, glaring. "I reckon I know dyed hair."

Before Billy could ask him how he knew so much about such sinful practices, Fentress looked at him pityingly. "She did dye her hair, Bill. Flournoy included that in his report." Fentress reached among the papers and pulled one toward him, glancing at it for confirmation. "Touched up as recently as twenty-four hours before death. Indications are it was a home job." He scowled at the paper. "He gets technical about the chemical agent, but says it's on the market as 'TintLox.' Lots of women use it," the investigator consoled him.

Bill didn't need consoling. It was just another indication of the way Penny had tricked him, lied to him unnecessarily. It wouldn't have made any difference to him whether her hair was naturally gilt-gold or touched up.

Gus was nodding with grim satisfaction over the coroner's confirmation of his direst suspicions when Fentress dropped the paper and turned to him. "In spite of the dyed hair and mutilated face you have positively identified your daughter?"

"Course I have. She was my daughter, warn't she?"

Fentress twitched impatiently. "That's what we're trying to determine. Accurately."

Gus looked sullenly at the desk and then up at Fentress. "Can't take a grieving father's own word about his daughter? It's just that I'm a poor working man without friends and money." Fentress' firm, authoritative cough cut short his lament. "Sure I'm sure. On account of the scar."

Bill, remembering Penny's smooth perfection, shook his head at Fentress. "She didn't have any scars." The little man glared at him. He twisted and bent over, pointing to the baggiest part of very baggy pants. "It's way up. Ran a splinter in her when she was ten. Cost me five dollars at the clinic to get her sewed up." He straightened suspiciously. "And anyway, how'd you know ain't she got a scar there?"

Bill wriggled uncomfortably. "I wouldn't—there. I mean, I never . . ." He floundered helplessly before Gus' outraged and accusing eyes.

Fentress hastily introduced them.

The little man's dour suspicions turned to cordiality. "Glad to know you." He looked Bill over with eyes that criticized the rumpled suit and made Bill conscious of yesterday's shirt. However, he seemed to allow him the privilege of eccentricity. "So you're the millionaire my Maggie married. She always said she would. Marry a millionaire, that is." He sighed dolefully. "Not that it done the poor girl much good." He shook his head lugubriously. "All that money and her lying there dead. Now she can't do none of the big things she planned. Like she was going to see I didn't want for nothing in my old age." He dragged out a rumpled and very grimy handkerchief and blew his nose with prolonged violence. "Poor girl, lying there dead."

Of all the inconsistencies and contradictions Bill had learned about Penny in past two days, Gus was by far the most improbable, the greatest contradiction. Penny had never even mentioned such a father, much less expressing this devotion Gus seemed to feel she had had. It made him acutely uncomfortable to watch the old man's grief because now he couldn't share it. So he was glad when Fentress cut across the emotionalism with brisk efficiency.

"Then you're satisfied that it is your daughter?"

Gus tweaked his nose violently with the dingy handkerchief. "Mister, I ain't satisfied with none of it. But that's my Maggie."

Fentress flushed and retreated behind formality. "Have you made a deposition to that effect?" As Gus peered at him over the dirty handkerchief, he simplified it. "A statement. Did you make a formal statement to the police that the body is that of your daughter?"

Gus blew his nose and studied the words as if he considered them a devious police trap. "I tole them that's my Maggie and they wrote it down and I signed it."

Fentress nodded approval. "And her teeth check with the dental charts you were kind enough to bring." He sighed with relief. "I guess that settles technicalities. We can hold the inquest tomorrow. At ten. Courtroom B. Both of you will please be there." He stood up, dismissing them.

Gus looked down at his sagging coat and baggy, grimed pants. "These here is all I got." He raised suddenly watery eyes to Bill. "If you ain't ashamed of me."

"We can get you a new suit first thing tomorrow morning," Bill told him in gruff sympathy, and then wondered what had happened to the five hundred he'd sent the old man. His fare had been less than fifty.

"There's stores open now," Gus suggested with wriggling eagerness. "We could stop by on the way to the mansion. You wouldn't want the servants seein' your father-in-law like this?"

Bill didn't bother to tell him the mansion was only a six-room house and the servants were nonexistent, except for Mrs. Harris who "did" for them on Tuesdays and Thursdays. He led Gus out to the MG and headed for home.

Gus was not to be sidetracked. "Yonder's a store. Open, too."

Bill parked the MG and saw Brady slide the police car into a space ahead. So he was still being trailed? Still a suspect?

Bill was so intent on working out the problem of his own involvement that he scarcely paid any attention to Gus until an harassed-looking salesman shook a lavender and green plaid coat directly under his nose.

"This may seem a bit youthful," he began bravely, only to bog down in a sigh, "but your friend said . . ."

Bill blinked away from the violent plaid. "No! Something dark. An oxford gray, maybe."

The salesman smiled his relief. "I think I've persuaded him that oxford gray is more suitable for a funeral." He nodded distractedly toward an electric blue affair that Gus was fingering with absorption.

The little man gave it an affectionate pat and smiled moistly up at Bill. "Perty, ain't it?"

"The oxford gray . . ." Bill began.

"Oh, I'm taking that." Gus clawed at the brilliant blue, hugging the sleeve to him. "But my Maggie wouldn't begrudge her poor old father a suit that's just to his liking." He sighed wistfully. "And her always telling me I'd not want for anything in my old age. Loved her old dad, she did." Gus went on describing how much his dear little Maggie loved her poor old Daddy while Bill arranged for a more sober blue cheviot. Gus stopped lamenting long enough to stare at it. "Looks kinda solemn, like I was figurin' on goin' to nothin' but funerals the rest of my life. My little girl woulda wanted her old Dad to be happy, once she come into a million or so."

While the oxford gray was being altered "to go," Bill steered Gus away from chartreuse and maroon sports shirts, striped blazers and vivid slacks to an assortment of white shirts, underwear and a few of the less intense ties. The wardrobe complete to hats and a pair of orange and black pajamas Bill couldn't wean his away from, they started for home, Gus with most of his new outfit stowed in a new pigskin bag tucked lovingly between his knees. He patted the upended bag. "Maggie always meant I should have nice things. Always meant to see I got 'em, once she got rich." He cut his rheumy eyes sidewise and his voice drooled gloom. "Don't know what I'll do now that Maggie's gone. Sorta lived on her hopes, I did."

By the time they were home Bill was fed up with the whining, sycophantic voice, the rheumy eyes and the greedy, thin-lipped mouth, and regretted the impulse that had led him to finance this trip. At the first opportunity he'd get rid of the old man.

Gus provided the excuse himself.

He swaggered in with his new suitcase, refusing to release it even to Bill, and set it down in the living room, peering around, disappointment and disapproval showing. "Kinda snappy but nothin' for a millionaire. My Maggie deserved better'n this, she did. And she'da seen her old Dad got a nice snug place, she would." He sneered at the modern coffee table. "Don't look like such a much."

Bill agreed with him. He'd told Penny the table wasn't good. Gus glanced incuriously at the over-glamorized photo of Penny on the mantel. "Who's the babe?"

"That's my wife, Penny. I mean, it's Maggie. Your Maggie." As Gus remained skeptical Bill added, "It doesn't look much like her, even as she was, and she must have changed considerably since you last saw her. She was sixteen then, I believe."

Gus swiveled back to the super-glamorized, super-sexed picture from which all resemblance to Penny had been retouched away. He sighed heavily. "So that's my little girl. My, she growed up beautiful!" He winked rheumy, pathetically pleading eyes. "Could I have this?"

"There's a better one upstairs." Bill reached for it, recalling Penny's inscription scrawled gushingly across the obvious expanse of bosom: "To My Darling Billie Boy from Your Penny." He writhed with embarrassment just remembering it.

"This here is the one I want." Gus grabbed the picture greedily, his eyes defensively watching Bill.

"Certainly." Bill shrugged and turned to answer the phone.

"She looks," Gus held off the picture, sighed, "like she's promising you things. Like she promised me that chicken farm." He smiled waveringly.

That was the solution, the way to get rid of Gus gracefully! Bill grinned amiably at Gus as he reached for the clamoring phone. "Don't worry, Mister Hutzler. You'll get your chicken farm. Just as soon as we can arrange it."

He hunched on both elbows, listening to the final whir of the phone before he heard Janet's voice, clear, sharp and furious.

"Bill, come down here at once! Immediately! They've arrested Miss Emily!"

Chapter XV

The scene in Fentress' office was not quite what Bill had expected. The furniture, including the new glass desk top, was intact and even the chairs were reasonably in order, but the personnel looked shattered. Casey and a uniformed policeman looked like men who had just lost an argument with a steamroller—not that they were actually battered but they had the dazed, uncertain stance of recent accident victims. Fentress, though reasonably calm, wore the stunned look of an auction bidder who has just learned he has bought a tiger but no cage.

Janet, from the fire in her eye, might well have been the tiger, a rather young and enticing-looking tiger in a tipsily raffish green that was most unbecoming but somehow hauntingly familiar. Bill blinked, trying to sort out the rest of this odd cast. There was Dick, who certainly had no business being here and looked as if he'd just realized it. The red-head, whom Bill remembered as having a temper and the improbable name of Candy Kane, looked cool and entertained in a gown that undoubtedly kept her cool and the public entertained. Belle Forbes (née Sadie Glutzman) seemed to be struggling to remember she was a lady without being up in her lines. Her role was further hampered, though "hampered" is hardly the word for it, by a costume consisting largely, but not too largely, of strategically placed spangles inadequately covered by a dingy red wrapper. Felix Whitsell, looking oddly unfinished without his briefcase, had plumped himself flatly in a chair to one side and midway between the officials and the odd assemblage, and was watching both sides with the bright alertness of a man about to referee a Davis Cup match. From behind a cloud of cigar smoke a stout man in a tuxedo was trying to share his amusement with a tall, sullen brunette in a metallic green gown that left little to the imagination except how it stayed up. Near them and obviously under guard of the stolid policeman behind his chair, a little man with a dead-white, cadaverous face twitched jerkily inside an oversized and much padded dinner jacket as he tried to watch everybody with darting venomous eyes.

Only Miss Emily was monumentally calm.

Casey began again, without hope of convincing anyone to explain things. He nodded toward Miss Emily. "She beat up a gangster."

"A gunsel," Miss Emily corrected. "And I . . ."

"When I got there," Casey rushed on, "she was sitting on him and holding up the joint with that." He pointed to a monstrous Luger on the desk. "And then . . ."

The stout man removed his cigar and waved away the smoke. "The Rendezvous is not a joint." By that Bill identified him as Ben Jade, owner of the club. "It's a respectable . . ."

Miss Emily outroared both of them. "I did not beat him up!" She folded heavy arms over the jittering medallion on her chest. "I pistol-whipped him!"

"Madam," Ben Jade regarded her over his cigar with amusement, "spanking a man with his own gun is not pistol-whipping—in the accepted sense." Jade shoved the cigar in his mouth, tucking in the edges of a smile. "Different, but effective."

"This is ridiculous!" Janet pounded the desk just under Fentress' nose. "That man," she pointed to the twitching little man, "tried to shoot us. All Miss Emily did . . ."

"They were trespassing." Ben Jade was amused but he was also clearing his legal skirts.

"Miss Emily was just going upstairs when this man . . ."

"To my private quarters," Jade murmured to his cigar, and then glanced admiringly at Miss Emily. "Though I would like to know how you took his gun away from him. Feeney has a reputation."

Miss Emily snorted. "Him?"

The twitchy little man jerked violently but subsided as Jade aimed his cigar at him. He snarled defensively.

"She clunked me."

"All she did was . . ." Janet had turned her guns on Ben Jade.

"We had gone to The Rendezvous," Miss Emily bellowed above everybody, "to see about girdles." At least, that's the way Bill heard it in the sudden quiet. "We had dinner," she nodded majestically to Jade, "a very acceptable dinner." Jade nodded back. "And we saw the floor show. Not so acceptable. Though you sing well." She nodded to the red-head, who looked surprised.

"After that, Miss Emily started backstage," Janet was calming down, trying to make the impossible sound logical. "She told me to wait for her, but when I saw her having an argument with the man at the curtained door . . ."

Miss Emily waved that aside with her stick. "I settled that. And then I stepped over his body and . . ."

"Body!" Fentress yelped, glaring at Casey. "You didn't tell me."

Casey shrugged. "He's in the hospital. Mild concussion."

"Then that man . . ." Miss Emily whirled on Feeney so that her medallion swept out in an arc and the twitchy

little man though half way across the room, ducked involuntarily. "He came at me with a gun. In my back." Miss
Emily, tried valiantly to reach around her ample person to
the spot but gave it up.

"I could see Miss Emily whirl—" Janet's words conjured for Bill a vision of an elephantine pirouette—"and
her big medallion swung out and struck him."

Feeney glowered venomously at Jade. "I tole you she
clunked me."

Miss Emily's hand swept out in a graphic swoop. "So I
grabbed his gun and then I turned him over my knee and
pistol-whipped him." She reared back and regarded Feeney
disparagingly. "Skinny little runt, isn't he? Shouldn't let a
thing like that carry a gun if he can't handle it."

Feeney's dead-white face turned green, his bleak black
eyes flattened to deadly opacity, and the twitching almost
jerked him out of his seat. Bill set himself to hurtle into
him if he moved, but the cop shoved Feeney deeper into
his chair.

"You shouldn't have said that, Mrs. Tilworthy," Jade
advised mildly. "Feeney has a reputation with a gun. He's
something of a champion."

Candy Kane leaned forward and lifted Miss Emily's
massive arm. "Meet the new champ."

Miss Emily gave the girl one startled glance and then
drew herself up massively. "He was fighting out of his
weight."

Fentress had recovered some of his aplomb and reached
across the desk, dragging the Lugar toward him by a pencil tip. "This may seem very amusing to you, Miss Emily—Mrs. Tilworthy. However, there are several charges
pending against you. I had you brought here rather than
to a station house in hopes we could straighten this out.
However, you have refused to cooperate. You still haven't

told me what you were doing at the time of this assault."

Miss Emily thumped her cane. "Charles Fentress! I told you I was going to the ladies' room. And when I'm going to the ladies' room, I brook no interference!"

Fentress sighed. "As I recall The Rendezvous, the ladies' room is clearly marked—and in the opposite direction."

Janet murmured sweetly, "Charles, you notice the oddest things."

Casey coughed loudly and Fentress flushed. Ignoring Janet, he waved the Luger at Miss Emily, realized what it was and lowered it hastily. "Just what were you doing at The Rendezvous?"

"Enjoying myself."

Fentress sighed and rested his head in his hand, shutting out the formidable bulk of Miss Emily. "I could hold you on charges until you decided to tell the truth." Ben Jade brushed past his twitchy henchman and stepped up to the desk. "You wouldn't get very far without complaining witnesses."

Fentress started up. "I've got complaining witnesses." He swept a hand out toward Belle, Candy, the girl in green and Feeney, stared at Jade's smile for an instant and dropped his hand. "Okay, Ben. So they're your employees and, if you say so, they're not complaining witnesses. I know how you work." He sank back in his chair. "I suppose I should be happy now if you don't sue me for false arrest."

Jade shrugged. "You know me. In a place like mine I don't want trouble and I don't want this kind of publicity." He bowed slightly to Miss Emily. "If you'll accept my apologies for a slight misunderstanding and be my guest at any time?" He left it an open question.

Miss Emily snorted. "You've got manners and you've got sense." She shook herself within the casement of her dress. "I accept."

Fentress waved his hand tiredly. "Let 'em go, Casey. All except Feeney. I'm holding him on an open charge." His eyes defied Jade to make something of that.

Instead of accepting the challenge Jade nodded affably. "I think you're wise. At least hold him till I can arrange to send him back to Detroit."

The little gunsel twitched himself half out of his chair, baring yellowed, crooked teeth in a feral snarl that died slowly under Jade's steady frown. The guard jerked him to his feet and led him away, mumbling, his opaque eyes turning back bitterly to Miss Emily.

Without another glance at his one-time gunman, Jade herded his employees out of the room firmly but without display. Bill felt he was watching an orderly and strategic retreat. Miss Emily drew herself up majestically.

"That Belle Forbes didn't recognize the hat," she announced triumphantly, as if that explained everything.

"Hat?" Fentress asked involuntarily, and then looked as if he wished he could drop the subject.

"That hat." With a vigorous sweep of her stick Miss Emily all but knocked the green hat from Janet's head.

Fentress managed to repress a shudder. "I've been looking at it ever since you came in, and frankly, Janet, it's the most unbecoming hat I've ever seen you wear."

"It's repulsive," Miss Emily stated flatly. "Especially on Janet."

"It's not mine." Janet swept it off, her eyes appealing to Bill. "It's one of Penny's." She held it out from her side gingerly.

"She wore it Friday afternoon. I checked." Miss Emily pivoted on Bill. "And don't blame Janet. I swiped it and made her wear it."

Fentress stared at the violently green hat considering it judicially. Unexpectedly he chuckled. "It was a wonderful idea, Miss Emily, except for one thing. Without her glasses, Belle Forbes couldn't recognize her own face in a mirror."

"Then it's probably the only thing that keeps her from having the screaming meemies." Miss Emily was not crestfallen. "I'll just have to think of something else. She didn't see Penny last Friday, you know. She couldn't know about those bruises."

"I've considered that possibility, especially after checking at the country club. About the tennis matches. No one noticed bruises." He shook his head resignedly. "She's probably lying, but the police will never get anyone in that crowd to admit it." He shrugged. "I can't see it's important, though. Especially since we can figure she's lying. She was just grabbing herself some limelight in a sensational murder case. We have that kind all the time."

"Was she?"

Bill felt a premonitory chill as Janet clutched his arm.

"Of course. You saw her act in here that day." Fentress tried to wipe out her suggestion, but even so his voice was uneasy.

"That's just it, Charles. I did see it. And that woman's no actress. She believed it. Somebody made her believe it."

"Who?"

Miss Emily marched to the door and turned heavily to look back.

"Somebody who wants to see Bill hanged."

Chapter XVI

The inquest was brief and businesslike.

A policeman testified crisply he had taken a call directing them to the residence of William Carey Taylor; another swore damply and perspiringly, as if he were reliving the moment, as to what they found there. Bill himself went on the stand and told quickly, with as little detail as possible, of his coming home to the murder, only they wouldn't let him use the word "murder" yet, so it was struck out. Then the police surgeon proved quite conclusively that Penny was dead "from repeated blows about the face and head that could not be self-inflicted," so that later they could legally call it murder. A fingerprint expert displayed enlarged samples of "the deceased's fingerprints, right and left hands," and told of matching prints found on the dresser, stair rail, kitchen table, highball glass and telephone in the Taylor residence, tied these neatly to F.B.I. files and through them traced a war plant in New Jersey and a Social Security card issued to "one Margaret Hutzler." Gus took the stand with itchy belligerence, identifying the Social Security card and a chart from a Newark dentist and stating that he had viewed the body and that it was his "Maggie that married a millionaire."

With Penny officially identified and pronounced dead, the jury, six "citizens without prejudice selected at random," filed out and returned promptly with its foregone verdict, "Willful murder at the hands of a person or persons unknown."

So much detail about so little! All they'd said was that Penny was now officially murdered and could be buried.

As the inquest broke up Bill shied away from sympathy, sliding out a side door to follow Fentress, who had given him a private signal to meet in the upstairs office.

Fentress, fortified behind his desk, smiled placatingly. "You didn't think much of it, did you, Bill? You probably feel we have sloughed off Penny's death. We haven't. The inquest is just a formality, and the simpler it is, the better. We don't expose our hand that way."

"Have you got a hand not to expose?" Bill felt angrily baffled and, though he knew it wasn't smart to antagonize Fentress, he couldn't help it.

Fentress sat down heavily, his hands spread. "Frankly, if we had laid our cards on the table, Taylor, that jury would have had to indict you—and I'd have to order your arrest. I'd rather go after stronger evidence—hanging evidence."

"Against me?"

"Against the killer, whoever he is." Fentress smiled apologetically. "Look, Bill, I'm not vindictive but neither am I lax, as you seem to believe because you feel this thing got sloughed off downstairs. I want to find the killer!"

"So do I." Bill leaned both fists on the desk. "And I'm working at it. So is Miss Emily."

"Miss Emily?" Fentress sat up in surprise. "Miss Emily!"

"Of course." Bill regretted his outburst, but he knew he had to go on. "When that gunman went after her, you don't think she was on her way to the ladies' room, do you?"

A smile twitched one corner of Fentress' mouth. "No."

"She was looking for evidence, digging into Penny's past."

"She doesn't need to. She already knows it. Very well." Fentress said it so quietly that Bill was already into his next sentence before he caught it.

"And she was going to . . . She what?"

"She knew about Penny's past. Perhaps better than any of us. And she hated her. With reason. Rightly or wrongly, Miss Emily believes Penny killed her son."

"That's crazy!"

"That's also a very sound motive for murder."

As Fentress outlined it, the tragedy of Freddie Tilworthy was sordid, miserable and brief. He had shot himself after an affair with Penny. As bald as that. A cheap affair and a suicide in a shabby hotel room in Pasadena. Fentress made it only too clear that Miss Emily had known of Penny's part in it, too. Old war horse that she was, Miss Emily hadn't taken the death of her only son easily. She had badgered the police, hired private detectives and gone out to Pasadena herself in her bitter, militant efforts to fight the woman who had ruined her son. But it had come to nothing except the ignominy of a verdict of suicide.

"But Penny was only a child," Bill protested. "Seventeen or so."

Fentress smiled his pity. "Keep your illusions, Bill. At seventeen some women are as old as Eve. Oh, the police had nothing against her—no records, even, except in connection with the suicide, but they knew her. Pasadena was overrun with Victory Girls in those days."

Bill shut away these unwanted pictures of Penny, though he knew he'd have to take them out again later and study them. But right now he concentrated on the present. On Miss Emily.

"You see," Fentress explained, "there's that phone call. Miss Emily couldn't have gotten it, Bill. Not at the time she said. Your wife was already dead then. Frankly, if it hadn't been for that call—or rather the fact that it was

Miss Emily who reported it—we'd probably have arrested you. It focused our attention on her and opened up other possibilities, but it's still not enough evidence, in itself, to justify arresting her." He smiled bitterly. "And arresting Miss Emily is going to take some doing. Not that she's immune. We brought her in once. We can do it again. But we're not going to move against her—or anybody—until we've got an airtight case." Fentress tilted back his chair, tenting his fingers. "We have also considered the possibility that she wants to draw our attention away from you. If you killed Penny—or she thought you did—you'd have her complete sympathy and all the protection she could give you. Undoubtedly, to Miss Emily, Penny's killer is a public benefactor."

Bill left with a perfunctory goodbye and drove home scarcely aware of Brady beside him.

Still in a muddle he went up the front steps, brushing past Gus on his furtive way out. He was staring vaguely at his house key as Brady lumbered up behind him.

"Pop just went scuttling off. What's the matter? Key won't fit?"

Bill shook himself. "Oh, it fits. It's just. . ."

"Sure." Brady nodded agreeably. "Your partner let himself in with a key this morning when he came to take you for the inquest."

"He's always had one. He lived here before I married."

"Sure. That's natural. Just forgot to return it." Brady turned the key over and over in blunt but agile fingers, examining it ingenuously.

"Then why are you so concerned about keys?" It was natural that Dick should have a key. Bill realized his voice was getting sharp and clamped down on it.

Brady grinned amicably. "Same reason you are. A guy that's friendly enough to bring along his own bottle of Scotch is friendly enough to have a key."

The idea sickened Bill, yet, knowing Penny as he now did, it seemed possible. "Only whoever brought the Scotch—and killed her—didn't necessarily need a key. Penny probably let him in, as she would any visitor."

"You got something there. A key ain't strictly necessary. If Penny's killer was friendly. Still it helps to know who had 'em." He tossed the key, let it fall almost to the floor and then snatched it. "Now that secretary of yours—what's-her-name?—Janet Hayden—she let herself in with a key. The night your wife was killed. To fix your supper."

He hadn't thought of that until this minute, but of course the police had. He tried to keep his face poker-still. "Oh, she probably used the set I keep at the office. A spare set. In my desk." That was true. I do keep a spare set down there because on the job I've lost my keys. So they can check and be damned to 'em. But another thought niggled at him. It wouldn't make any difference where Janet had gotten the key: the fact remained that if she could get a key at six she could have had one at nine in the morning.

Damn them! Couldn't they leave him a little faith in anyone!

Brady finally handed the key back. "Those keys at your office, now. Could Felix Whitsell have gotten 'em?"

"I suppose so," he answered dully. "Anybody could've. We're in and out. The office is never locked during the day."

"Is that gonna be the official explanation of the telegram, too? Anybody could get in to send it? Like Whitsell, maybe?"

Bill was astonished. "Why Felix? He's harmless." Then he grasped at the idea. "Yes. Anybody could have sent it, couldn't they? Just anybody." Then he hated himself for having to grasp at such feeble straws. And he hated Brady for putting him in that position.

Brady seemed to sense that the casual camaraderie of their enforced companionship was gone, at least temporarily, for he went back to his post outside, something he hadn't done since that first night. Bill tried to work on the Bedford plans but the feel for them was gone. So he welcomed the ring on the phone. It was Miss Emily with an invitation to join her at The Rendezvous. She was taking up Ben Jade's offer of the night before. He picked up Brady, apparently unperturbed by the shift of role. But he was surprised on arriving at their destination.

Bill explained, "Miss Emily asked me to meet her here. On business."

Brady grinned. "Business? Or monkey business?" His smile faded. "Or police business?"

"Miss Emily's business, Jim. I guess it's no secret she wants to find out why Belle lied, and Fentress will probably be grateful if she does. He admits he'll never get anything out of these people."

Brady nodded to the canopy. "You're so right. Jade nor none of his people like cops. Not even to come in for a beer." He sighed gustily. "And don't try going out the back door. It's watched."

So Fentress hadn't given up on Jade's people as easily as he'd thought. Bill flipped a hand at Jim. "I'll send you out that beer." And he entered the club, almost deserted in this off-hour. He ordered Brady's beer from an astonished waiter and then asked for Jade. The waiter seemed uneasy but passed him on to another who led him across the barren room, through a curtained door and up the stairs to Jade's office.

Jade, his massive face coldly calm, was seated behind an immense desk barren except for a heavily handsome ashtray which was just then being threatened with swoops of Miss Emily's silver-knobbed stick.

"Blast it, Ben, I know it was a gentleman's agreement. And by thundering wallupuses, I've come to see you pay off. Now. Today."

Jade settled back grimly, eyeing Miss Emily. He spoke around his aggressively tilted cigar. "Then why send this creep to stooge among my people? Everybody's upset. I don't like it."

Miss Emily drew herself to monumental dignity. "I don't send stooges of any kind, and most certainly not creeps."

Jade sucked on his cigar thoughtfully, let his eyes drift sidewise to where the girl in green sat sullenly, only she was in red this time. He seemed to study her lovely, immobile face for a clue. Suddenly he yanked out the cigar like a champagne cork and words came bubbling after. "Bosh! Police don't send such obvious stooges. This guy was a real creep, a sniveling, ratty character that claimed to be Penny's father."

Bill was amazed. "Gus was here?"

Jade squinted across his desk, as if he'd seen him for the first time, but Bill suspected that Ben rarely missed what was going on. "That you, Taylor? You know this creep, Gus? Yeah. Said his name was Gus Hutzler. Claimed to be Penny's father, showing a picture of her around and sniveling over it. A phony if I ever saw one." Jade regarded his cigar fondly, like a man who knows the genuine and appreciates it. "A very repulsive character."

Bill could agree with that. "He is. But Gus is really her father."

"Hooey!" The sullen girl beside Ben spoke for the first time since Bill had known her. "Also, phooey! Penny was an orphan. Me, I know her for years." Her voice was a flat, dead Brooklynese.

That the girl should speak at all seemed to astonish Ben as much as what she said. He hitched his whole chair around to look at her. "You knew Penny?"

"We was kids together. We went to the same school."

Ben rumbled deep in his big body. "Who says you went to school?"

"So I'm a dope. So it was a reform school. But Penny was an orphan then. You don't grow fathers later."

Chapter XVII

"When was this?" Ugly as it was, it was a new piece to the mosaic of Penny's past. He avoided the sympathy in Miss Emily's eyes and concentrated on the girl. "I mean, when were you in this school?"

"Which time?"

"The time you knew Penny."

"She wasn't Penny then. She was Ellen Pierce."

"All right. When did you know Penny as Ellen Pierce?"

"Let's see." The sullen brunette stared at Ben's cigar for inspiration. "A long time ago. I was thirteen." Her immobile face lighted. "But I looked older."

"When was this?" Bill felt he could strangle the girl, she took so long getting to the point.

She looked at him with surprised eyebrows. "All the time I look older." She thought about that for a moment. "Except now."

It took time, but between them Jade and Bill got the story from her. She had known Penny as Ellen Pierce, an incorrigible, in Brooklyn, where both of them had served time in a reform school from which Penny, or Ellen, had run away when she was about fifteen. She had seen Penny several times in the intervening twelve years. No, there was no mistake. Penny Wise was Ellen Pierce. The sullen girl made that clear. She was stupid, but she knew a good line when she had one and she stuck with it. "She was an orphan then. You don't grow fathers later."

Exasperated but convinced, Bill sat back. "Then why should Gus claim to be her father?"

The sullen girl shrugged. "I dunno. He ain't her father, but maybe he was her 'Daddy.' Could be. She had a lot of 'em."

"Her 'Daddy?'"

"They got a rule says a man can't live with a kid fifteen-sixteen." Her shrug implied how silly she considered this particular rule. "So she calls him 'Daddy.' Could be. Now he's stuck with it."

Bill made for the door without realizing how grim he looked, only knowing that a sudden silence had fallen. As he reached the door Miss Emily quivered into vast motion, but he waved her back to her chair.

"Please. I just feel sick."

He almost ran out to the MG, and there felt better with fresh air in his lungs.

"Bad news?" Brady's sympathy was warm and quick. Bill slid into the seat, breathing deeply. "No worse than the rest, but . . ." He told Brady about Gus and these new suspicions. Brady shifted to look at him, listening patiently.

"So he's a phony? Fentress will want to talk to him." He was already getting out of the car. "I'll bring him in. Joe said he was headed for Folsom's." He pointed with his thumb. "Down there a couple of blocks." Joe, Bill figured, was the plainclothesman watching The Rendezvous.

Folsom's office was in an old building that had been hastily revitalized for the high-rent boom with cheap, bright paint. Nothing, however, had been done about the clattery old elevator or fifty years of tired odors. The office itself was a double cubbyhole. An outer cubicle was a reception room with a home-painted desk and chair, a slat bench with its dark varnish worn to the wood in well-sat spots, and a display of theatrical photographs that seemed to consist almost entirely of tap dancers in the same exaggerated pose with a top hat, and girls as near nude as the law allows, all flowingly inscribed. Bill swept the picture-decorated wall swiftly but didn't see one of Penny. Through a door he could see the inner cubicle and a man's hands jamming a folder back into a battered file cabinet. As Brady closed the outer door noisily, a thin, irritated voice called out, "No casting today."

"We're looking for a character." Brady lounged against the inner door and shoved it wide open.

"Well!" Irritation dropped from the voice. "Come in."

As Brady crowded into the cubicle Bill could see a young man pressing his shoulders against the file cabinet to give Brady's bulk room to pass. On second look, the man was only theatrically young, as if he hoped somebody would refer to him as "Boy Genius." Brady shoved by and the theatrically young man sidled into a chair cramped between desk and cabinet, his hands restlessly brushing the center of the desk clear of torn scraps of paper. Pieces fluttered to the floor, unnoticed. It was that kind of office. The youngish man bobbed his head briskly. "A character, eh?" He seemed to see Bill for the first time. "Can you find a chair?"

I've seen that guy before, Bill thought. Sure. At Caswell. And at the inquest.

Bill swung the receptionist's chair around and sat in the doorway while Folsom gave all his attention to Brady. "So you're looking for a character actor, eh?" He hitched his chair around importantly and moved his knees out of the way to open a file drawer. Over his bent head Brady winked at Bill. Folsom slapped a thin file folder on the desk. "Just what type?"

Brady rubbed his chin, working out the words. "Small. Scrawny. Fifty—sixty, maybe. Thin gray hair. Ratty face. Sniffles."

Folsom nodded. "The Raymond Hatton type. I've got just the man." He flipped open the folder and glanced up. "What sort of part does he play?"

"A stinker." Brady reached across, took the file and riffled hastily through a sheaf of stylized photos.

He brushed the last one aside impatiently. "Cut it, Folsom. I'm looking for Gus Hutzler."

"Hutzler?" Folsom paused as if listening to his own voice say the name. Suddenly he scrabbled the photos together and shut the folder. "He's not registered with us. I don't know any . . ." He jerked upright, staring past Brady, whipping his eyes around to peer at Bill. "Hutzler!" His eyes widened and his almost patrician nose flared angrily. "You're not a producer!" He swung around and thrust the folder peevishly down among a scant dozen others. "I don't know Gus Hutzler, but if you're police, you ought to." He tapped a folded newspaper on his desk. "I read that he's the father of that girl who was killed."

"Your client, Penny Wise."

Folsom kicked the drawer shut irritably and sneered at Brady. "So she was my client—once." His eyes said, So what of it?

Brady's sausage finger stirred the pile of torn scraps on the desk. Several more pieces fluttered to the floor. This time Folsom eyed them with fascination.

"You were tearing up her pictures." Brady tapped the torn bits.

Bill looked closer. From one, upturned, Penny's face, retouched and glamorized, peered up at him. Folsom stretched out an elegant finger and flipped it face down. "Unfinished business." He laughed briefly. "Or maybe I should say, finished business. I was clearing out my files."

"About Gus Hutzler," Brady reminded him. "He was headed for here about an hour ago."

Folsom shrugged. "He never got here. And if he's like your description, I'm just as glad. 'Specially if he's involved with Penny."

"You didn't like Penny?" Brady said it with amiable surprise.

"I've got to like clients?" He shrugged. "Penny spelled trouble. In a business way," he added hastily. "Strictly. Temper, canceled dates, broken contracts." He spread his hands expressively. "She'd drop a contract date for any man that came along—with money."

Bill's hands crunched down on the crisp fragments of paper and he levered himself on knotted fists, starting for Folsom. But Brady somehow got between them, shouldering him back. Bill jammed his clenched fists deep into his pockets without realizing that he still clutched a handful of scraps. "I'm all right," he muttered at Brady, subsiding into his chair. "But I still can't get used to the idea that everybody knew Penny was cheap—everybody but me."

Folsom tittered. "Your friend's impulsive."

"Maybe I shoulda let him slap you. He's her husband."

"Penny's?" Folsom swiveled in his chair to study Bill. "So you're Penny's husband?" He gave it plenty of surprise, even with his eyebrows.

"You knew him all right." Brady stood up, preparatory to leaving. He leaned across and flipped open the folded paper. Bill's picture, two columns wide, stared up at them. "Let's go." Brady grabbed Bill's arm and they were out of the office and in the rachitic elevator before Bill recovered from his astonishment.

"Why not stay there and ask him . . ."

"Ask him what?" Brady lifted his shoulders, dropped them. "He's been asked—by experts."

"Then why the play with the paper?"

"It gives him something to worry about, if he's got anything to worry him. Next time he'll come up with honest answers."

"What sort of answers?"

Brady looked blank. "How should I know? I don't know the questions yet."

On the way to the lobby Brady tried to question the operator, a man as ancient and decrepit as the elevator, about Gus. It was futile. On the ground floor he went back to the solitary pay phone. "Gotta report on that girl's story about Gus." He squeezed himself into the booth and shut the door. A few minutes later he wrenched himself out, mopping his forehead and staring past Bill.

"What's wrong, Jim?"

"Maybe that fancy jerk upstairs is right. Maybe Gus never got here!"

"Never got here? He had scarcely two blocks to come."

Brady knuckled his hat back perplexedly. "Sure. He tells everybody at The Rendezvous he's headed for Folsom's. Just two blocks to go. And somewhere along the way he gives his shadow the slip. Now Fentress wants Gus— bad. Real bad."

Chapter XVIII

Bill decided to return to The Rendezvous to apologize to Miss Emily for walking out on her. "After all, she arranged this meeting on my account," he explained to Brady, who settled down in the MG for another patient wait.

Without the help of a waiter Bill found his way up to Jade's office. As he opened the door sound blasted out at him—Miss Emily's second best bellow. Her really prime effort would have rattled the door on its hinges.

"So you never saw this hat before!"

As Bill stepped in Ben nodded absently to a chair by his desk. The sullen girl looked up with a faint twitch of a smile and then turned back to stare in fascination at Miss Emily flourishing the hideous green hat under Belle Forbe's red and swollen nose. Belle gulped noisily. "It's a beautiful hat."

"It's an awful hat! But you can't help noticing it." The redhead, elbow on her knee, her thumb rigidly supporting her chin while she gnawed on her index finger, followed the flourishing hat with astonished eyes. She rocked her head in agreement. "A girl in that hat would be as conspicuous as Lady Godiva at a Baptist Revival."

Belle sniffled. She appealed to Ben Jade. "You'd think I stole it or sump'n, an' I never seen it before."

"Then you never saw Penny on Friday!" Miss Emily slammed the hat down on Jade's desk like evidence before a jury.

Belle blubbered, heaving her conspicuous bosom and writhing in her chair. She pouted at Miss Emily. "An' I thought you really wanted to talk about girdles."

Miss Emily continued the attack. "Who put you up to that lie?"

For a long moment Belle regarded her with red-rimmed eyes, her lower lip thrust out rebelliously. She rocked on her heavy buttocks and hugged flabby arms under her bosom in an effort to maintain her secret. "It wasn't really truly a lie," she whimpered childishly, "so it don't make no difference. It was the truth. He seen them bruises."

The redhead sighed, slapping her knees in exasperation. "If you were Hydra, you'd have a hole in each head." She jerked her chin upward. "Go ahead, now. Make like a canary."

Belle heaved herself around, grieving bovinely at her friend for this new betrayal. "If Phil says he seen 'em, he seen 'em. That's why I . . ." She stopped so suddenly her false teeth kept on moving from sheer inertia. She clicked them shut and tongued them back into place with a fearsome contortion of her raddled face.

The redhead appealed to the ceiling. "That lets the cat out of the bag."

"Who's a bag?" Belle demanded in one final flare before she crumpled soggily. "I hadda. I hadda. He'da fired me if I didn't." Her eyes pleaded with Miss Emily. "An' where's a girl like me gonna get another job? I'm old and fat and tired." She folded nearly double in her abandon to grief.

Miss Emily thumped her stick impatiently once before she sighed. "I don't think Phil Cameron is going to fire you." She glared at Ben Jade. "Is he?"

Ben regarded his cigar thoughtfully. "We'll find a spot for Belle."

"A permanent place," Miss Emily amended firmly. "And now I'd like to talk to this Phil Cameron."

"Cameron?" Bill asked perplexedly. "What motive could he have?"

"Bill, I'll be blamed if I know. But I certainly intend to ask him. He could have a dozen motives." She glared at Ben. "How about it?"

Jade shrugged. "As soon as he returns. He's gone to get Feeney released and put him on the train for Detroit." The big restauranteur sighed. "Miss Emily, you certainly have disrupted things."

"I usually do." Miss Emily sighed with vast satisfaction. "And while we're waiting, let's eat." She beamed at Ben Jade. "This is on me."

"You're my guest," Jade insisted, rising.

Miss Emily chortled. "That's rash. I didn't get this figure on toast and black coffee."

Jade glanced down at his own massive frame and grinned. "I opened a restaurant so I could afford this. Come on, girls." He twinkled at Miss Emily. "Usually I don't do that. When I'm out to enjoy good food I don't like beautiful women around. Beautiful women are the bane of the dinner table. Their diets won't let them pay due attention to good food, and their vanity won't let anybody else." Nevertheless he ushered the sullen brunette out gallantly.

On the way to the dining room Miss Emily took Bill's arm, pulling him into loping step with her own erratic progress. "I'm not being as flippant as I seem, Bill. But life goes on and people eat. I'm not neglecting things. We've gotten to Cameron. If we can't make him talk, the police can. It's a step."

Bill nodded and told her about Gus. As he talked he fumbled for a cigaret, dredging up the scraps of torn photographs he had inadvertently clutched from Folsom's desk. He was looking around for a place to throw them when a fragment of writing caught his eye.

Bill recognized it. He'd seen it often enough and every time it had embarrassed him. *"To My Darling Billie Boy, from Your Penny,"* had been scrawled across the display of bosom in the photograph Penny had kept on the mantle. This was part of that inscription.

Miss Emily flicked the paper from between his suddenly nerveless fingers. She glared at it. "Sickening twaddle. I remember it on your mantle. Always did think . . ." She broke off, glaring. "You said you gave that sluttish thing to Gus. Where'd you get this?" She shook the fragment at him.

"Folsom's . . ." He was already running down the hall. "And it shouldn't have been there!"

Bill caromed off an indignant patron and banged out the door, clambering into the MG, nudging Brady into his corner. As he started the car he saw Dick Barnes sidling into the alleyway that led behind The Rendezvous to the kitchen quarters, the stage door and, according to rumor, to Jade's private gambling den. It was unlike Dick to gamble and his secretive sidling was completely out of character, but Bill put that aside to sketch in for Brady the significance of finding the fragment. By the time he had finished he was drawing up in front of the building where Folsom had his office.

"So Folsom lied?" Brady nodded grimly. "Well, we'll get him."

They didn't. The office was unlocked but dark and empty, and their floor by floor search was necessarily superficial, but by the time they returned to the ground floor they were sure Folsom was gone.

Miss Emily, her stick militantly lifted, waited at the bottom of the stairs that spiraled around the clattery elevator. "I followed you. Nobody's slipped down since I've been here." She lowered her stick and leaned heavily on it. "There's still the basement," she suggested, and then eyed the rickety elevator with a sigh. "Not that I'd risk my neck in that thing. I'll wait here."

Bill and Brady went through the damp, musty basement, turning on dim bulbs without even seeing traces of recent footprints in the thick, oily dust. They were fumbling their way back to the stairs when Bill heard Miss Emily saying loudly, "You fool, the police are all around this building, so put down that gun." Her stick thumped commandingly just above their heads. "Put down that gun and no one will hurt you."

Bill started forward only to be jerked to a stop by Brady's barring arm.

A thin, reedy laugh. "No cops. I followed you from Jade's."

Feeney!

With a caution and silence Bill wouldn't have believed possible, Brady glided up the first few steps, angling his head to peer upward through the grill work of the ancient elevator shaft, his gun snaking between the bars for a shot at the hoodlum, above and to their right. Even from where Bill was forced to wait he could see it was an impossible shot. Miss Emily's broad back was between them and the slight figure of the gunman. Brady crept up a few steps, working his way toward a turn in the stairs and a possible clear shot.

Miss Emily went on talking. "All right, Feeney, since you're going to kill me, do you mind telling me why you murdered Penny?"

"What!" The slight figure twitched but the Luger remained steady. "Me? Kill Penny? That's a laugh! That's for sure a laugh." To prove it, Feeney sniggered. "That murder—that's my meal ticket. My social security." He sniggered again and then burst into high, sustained giggles. "That murder's gonna keep me in style—the rest of my life."

The stomach-shaking crash of a gunshot in the closed, narrow space jerked Bill away from his grip on the grill. Through the bars he could see Feeney rise delicately on his toes and balance for two mincing steps before he bent backward in an arc that was agonizing just to watch, then spiral downward on one crumpling knee, land soddenly and lie still.

Miss Emily raised her stick in a salute toward the back of the hall. "Nice shooting! Thanks." Somewhere back along the hall a door slammed.

The second sound roused Bill and he hurtled up the stairs, passing Brady who was looking vacantly at his Police Positive and shaking his head.

"Miss Emily!" Bill stumbled into the hall. "Are you all right?"

Miss Emily gulped. "Stop asking foolish questions." She took an overhand grip on her stick and putted the Luger well down the hall. "He looks dead, but you never can tell."

Bill knelt beside the crumpled gunman. "He's dead, all right. Brady got him."

"Brady, my eye!" Miss Emily aimed her stick down the corridor. "Somebody down there shot him."

Brady came to the head of the stairs, breathing heavily, still holding his gun. "That's right. I didn't get in a shot. Must have been Kernak. This is his beat."

Brady aimed a flashlight down the dark corridor. It lighted the cracked and peeling back door which the landlord hadn't gotten around to painting yet. The corridor, from end to end, was bleakly empty.

Chapter XIX

Miss Emily was the first to get the full implication of that empty corridor. "That was no cop. That was Penny's killer! Feeney knew who it was." She looked down at the dead gunman. "Poor, twisted little man. He thought he had something good. He was just saying it would keep him the rest of his life." Her stick thumped the linoleum savagely. "Come to think of it, he was right. But it was an awful short life." She tapped Feeney's foot lightly with her stick. "Little man, you should have gone to Detroit."

Brady was just returning from a hasty check on the back door, shaking his head. "Nobody there. An alley. Got clean away." He scowled at Miss Emily. "You didn't see who it was?" For answer Miss Emily pointed down the dark corridor and Brady nodded. "Couldn't recognize my own mother ten feet away."

Bill didn't remember, but he supposed he said the appropriate things, if there are appropriate things to be said about a murder victim to *his* prospective victim. It seemed to him he just stood there, staring down at Feeney's blank face and sprawled body, while Brady went back to the phone booth and started the complex machinery of official investigation.

By the time Brady got back Dick had charged into the corridor from the street door, taken one horrified look, turned palely green and whirled to block off the redhead and Belle Forbes, coming in behind him. Over his shoulder he was explaining to Bill, "I came as soon as the girls told me where you were headed. I didn't think it was safe."

Miss Emily looked up from her long study of Feeney, "It wasn't. For him."

The redhead peered around Dick's shoulder. "He went tearing off and we followed him. In a cab. Omigod, it's waiting!" She saw Feeney sprawled on the floor, nodded at him. "Nothing trivial, I hope," she managed flippantly, but shivered, withdrawing behind Dick. Belle was wailing noisily on the general principle that wailing was probably expected of her.

The three were thrust aside as Ben Jade plowed through and came to a halt several feet from the body. He reached for his cigar which wasn't here. "So he got it." He located a fresh cigar and began to unpeel the cellophane. "Phil just phoned me Feeney slipped off the train, so I came to warn you." He nodded to Miss Emily and unexpectedly grinned. "Should have known I needn't bother. For a lady you do the damnedest things I ever saw."

"I'm the damnedest lady you ever saw. But I didn't do this."

Outside, a siren sounded, and the corridor was suddenly full of organized bustle that swept Bill and Miss Emily into a back office full of broken pinball machines and three dilapidated chairs. But not before Bill had seen Janet trying to crowd in the front door, waving frantically to Miss Emily, only to be pushed back to the street.

Miss Emily regarded the office with distaste and the chairs with suspicion. Then her eye lighted on a pinball machine whose only defect seemed to be a missing leg. She had lighted up three near-nudes and a rather impossible battleship and run up a preposterous score by the time Fentress, Casey and Brady came in. Together they went over the story of the shooting three times, once for a quick run-through, once for details and the third time to convince Casey that Bill hadn't somehow managed to do the shooting. Casey's bleak look at Brady, Bill's best witness, seemed to say his fellow officer had somehow betrayed him.

Fentress picked up the original reason for their convergence on Folsom's office, the scrap of photograph that proved Gus had been there and Folsom had lied about it. "So he did come here?"

Casey growled in his harsh monotone. "When I see the guy that let that little weasel slip away I'll bust him back to patrolman and put him so far out in the sticks it'll take radar to find him. Soon as he knew Gus had given him the slip, he shoulda went right to Folsom. He knew he was headed there."

Fentress defended the man mildly. "He knew Gus *said* he was going to Folsom's. Don't worry, I've got men out now looking for both Gus and Folsom."

Casey shook his head angrily, like a man ridding himself of a bee. "We had men lookin' for Feeney and look what happened."

Fentress sighed. "I know." He turned to Miss Emily. "Incidentally, whatever made you think Feeney had killed Mrs. Taylor?"

Miss Emily straightened in astonishment. "I never thought he had a thing to do with it. I was just stalling."

The investigator looked faintly ill. "Stalling? You accused a man with a gun of murder? By rights he should have started shooting."

Miss Emily snorted. "Nonsense. The man had a guilty conscience."

"That's just what I'm saying. A man with a guilty conscience . . ."

"When you accuse a man with a guilty conscience of something he didn't do, he'll fall all over himself explaining how he didn't do it. I needed that time for Brady and Bill to get here. At least now you can stop suspecting Bill and me."

"Miss Emily, I never suspected you."

"Of course you did. You suspected from motives alone. What you didn't know was that I'd forgiven Penny. I made a bargain that I wouldn't hurt her—as long as she kept Bill happy. And, blind and bumbling as he is, that could have been forever."

That's me. Bill swallowed huskily. Blind and bumbling, an oaf.

"I gave Ralph Taylor my word."

Bill jerked himself to attention. "Uncle Ralph knew about Penny?"

Miss Emily caught his arm fondly. "Your Uncle Ralph knew everything about everybody that counted in his life. That's what made him a great man—and a rich one." She tugged at his arm. "Let's go, Bill."

He let her lead him down the hall while he was trying to adjust to this new idea of Uncle Ralph. He pulled mulishly to a halt just inside the grimy entrance doors. "If he knew about Penny, why didn't he tell me?"

"You were in love. Would you have listened? It would only have made a breach between the two of you, and Ralph loved you. Besides, you didn't give anybody much of a chance. Just up and did it. Anyway, I doubt if he knew the whole story till afterward, or he'd have bought her off."

Three months ago—up to a week ago—Bill would have laughed at that, but now . . . Yes, Penny, as he now knew her, could probably have been bought off. Not cheaply, but bought off.

Outside, the ambulance clanged impatiently and swung into traffic, pulling away. Miss Emily dragged Bill with her to the street and watched it. She pounded angrily on the sidewalk with her stick. "And it's not finished yet! Somebody else has got to die."

"Somebody else?" He felt stupid echoing her words. "Who?"

"Who?" Miss Emily snuffled with what, in a lesser person, might be mistaken for emotion. "Who do you suppose? You!"

Bill stared after her rigid, uncompromising back as she stumped toward the ark-like Packard. He climbed into the MG beside a glum Brady and cautiously eased it through the gaping crowd to follow her.

Outside The Rendezvous Ben Jade had herded his crowd into a compact little group, but he hadn't yet succeeded in getting them into the club. Janet, Dick, the redhead, Belle Forbes and the sullen girl were still speculating on the shooting. Janet whipped away from the group to greet Miss Emily, and the others turned to stare. Dick sprang forward to help her out and barely dodged her violent lunge. Jade watched the impetuous descent with awed approval before he came forward to offer his massive arm. "Is there anything I can do?"

Miss Emily nodded. "I'd still like that dinner, and you can tell me where Ken Folsom would hole up and why was Cameron looking for Feeney—with a gun?"

"Dinner is waiting. I don't know about Folsom, but Phil wouldn't . . ." Jade reached for his cigar, stopped, startled by his own thoughts. He shook his head. "At least, I don't think he would. Unless he had some reason of his own."

"Somebody had a very good reason. Feeney knew who killed Penny Taylor. If I just knew where Folsom is . . ." Miss Emily stomped toward the club entrance.

The redhead whistled softly. "Could be the audition room."

Bill whirled on her. "The audition room? Where is it?"

She wrinkled up her nose at him and then glanced at Dick. "The girls call it that. It's a cabin where he 'auditions' girls, his private little racket. It's supposed to be a deep dark secret, but every showgirl in town knows it. He rents it under the name of 'Leslie.'"

"Where is it?"

The redhead cut her eyes around at him and back to Dick. Finally she grinned and swung back to Bill. "Sure, even I fell for his line about a fat part in a New York musical and went for a reading. But he and I couldn't see eye to eye."

"Do you know how to get there?"

The redhead laughed abruptly. "Do I? I know every step of the way—coming back." Under his steady scrutiny she sobered. "Take State 47 to Bellow's Crossroads, take a sand-clay road to your right to a church at a fork. Turn left on a gravel road, and watch that gravel. It'll ruin a girl's shoes. And then . . ."

Three minutes later he had it all down and was piling into the MG when Dick caught his arm. "I'd like to go, too, Bill. I've got a score to settle with Folsom about those auditions."

One leg inside the sports car, Bill stopped. "So it's like that, huh?" He peered across Dick's shoulder at the redhead.

"It's like that," Dick assured him solemnly.

Bill felt curiously elated. If Dick was in love with the pert, saucy redhead it explained many things, not the least of which was his constant skulking around The Rendezvous. He clapped him on the shoulder, shoving him back. "Brady and I sort of fill this thing, and I need Brady along to make it official, but you can follow." Knowing the speed of the MG, Bill doubted that, but he didn't explain. He wanted to find Folsom himself.

Bill felt alert, alive, for the first time since Penny's death. This was action and he knew how to handle action.

He whirled the MG away from the curb, explaining to Brady as they went, "And Miss Emily's phoning Fentress. Reinforcements are coming."

They said little as the tiny sports car whipped through the night, eating up the miles. Finally Brady pointed to a signpost hunched drunkenly against a corner of rail fence. "Leslie. That's the name she said he used up here."

Bill braked and wheeled the MG over a humped roll, of earth and on to twin ruts winding along a snakelike ridge that dropped sharply on each side to a scraggly growth of cut-over pines.

A huge boulder seemed to careen out of the night, to loom totteringly over them, and Bill twisted the wheel frantically before he realized it was an optical illusion, a trick of the swinging, bouncing headlights. The rock over-hung the road but it was permanent and fixed. He edged around it, slowing.

"Maybe we should walk from here. Surprise him."

Brady grunted, easing back into his seat. "If he's up here, he's already seen the headlights. Just keep going." The little car jounced sidewise and he moaned. "And he comes here for fun?"

The track leveled off there, and Bill swung the car so that its brilliant headlights fanned across the little pla-teau. He almost missed the dingy, rundown shack half hidden by scrub pine and camouflaged by its own dun-colored slab siding and sagging roof line. He swung back to center the headlights on it.

"Just hold it there." Brady stood up, Police Positive in his hand. He was already stepping out as Bill pulled the car to a halt.

Bill started to scramble out, but Brady's big hand shoved him back. Caught off-balance, he sat heavily. "What's the idea?" Angrily Bill started up again, and Brady sighed.

"You're a good chauffeur but you're no policeman. You got no rights here. And me, I want to get Folsom."

"So do I." Bill fumbled under the dash where he knew Uncle Ralph had kept an automatic in a clip, came up with it and stepped out beside Brady. "Let's go."

"He could sue you for all them millions—if we're wrong," Brady cautioned.

"And seeing we're out of the city, he could get you busted. What're we waiting for?"

"Take it easy." Brady grinned at him, pushing him. "No need to be targets." They slid behind the slight protection of the car and Brady bellowed into the night, "This is the police! Come out with your hands up!" He repeated it, waited a moment and bellowed again. He glanced at Bill. "Either he ain't here or he ain't coming out. You slip down in them pines and come up that way." He pointed to a slight shoulder of hill. "And I'll go around the other side. If he comes out this way, he runs into the lights and we spot him. Okay?"

Bill nodded and slid off to the right, skidding on the pine tags as he reached the trees, sliding and rolling down the slight incline. Then he was on his feet, crouched and trotting toward the shack, gun easy in his hand, his wrist loose.

Soon the shack was just above him, propped on the near side on stilted, ungainly legs. He could see, against the sky, the sagging skeleton of crooked back stairs and the squarish blot of a miniature porch. Still there was no movement inside.

He worked his way around to the foot of the stairs and could see the lighter oblong of glass inset in the back door where the car lights shone through the house. He started up the stairs, stopped, listened, leaning against one of the stilts. He could hear movement, the sound of footsteps, cautious, sliding. He breathed easier and started up again. They were outside, approaching the shack. Brady.

He crept up the few remaining stairs and was reaching for the doorknob when he heard the rush of Brady's feet across the front porch and the crash as his shoulder hit the front door. Almost together they hurtled into the room from opposite sides. Brady's flashlight stabbed out, centered an instant on Bill, almost blinding him, and whipped away, circling the room. Still blinking from the sudden light, for an instant, Bill didn't see what made Brady gasp.

Bill shook his head, opened his eyes and stared into Gus' sly, furtive grin. In the hard, bare light of the flash his face looked even grimier and grayer than usual and his eyes held a more malicious stare—without winking.

Gus was quite dead.

Chapter XX

Brady flicked the light away from the malicious, dead eyes and swept the shoddily furnished room, centered it on a curtained doorway and flicked it off. Bill could tell from the tight breathing and soft shuffle of feet that Brady was moving toward the curtained door. Just as his eyes were getting accustomed to the dim haze of the car's headlights filtered through the shuttered window—enough to see Brady's bulk—he had slipped through the curtain and was gone. A moment later he saw the swift, careful probe of the flashlight beyond the curtain and Brady clumped back. "Nobody there."

Bill clicked on the naked electric bulb hanging from the middle of the ceiling and looked back at Gus slouched in a faded and tattered morris chair. The harsh, yellowish glare didn't improve the dead face, and he almost switched it off again. Instead he came to stand in front of the grimy little man, studying him. One gnarled fist resting on the arm of the chair still clutched a tall, half-empty glass of pale amber, probably the remnants of a highball.

"He wasn't expecting it."

"Most of us don't."

"I mean, it looks like he was having a friendly visit. Or thought he was. Until somebody shot him." Bill pointed to the highball glass, a bottle of cheap whiskey on the table

and a chipped vegetable dish of water that had probably once been ice cubes from the elderly Frigidaire in the
corner.

"Yeah." Brady bent over and sniffed at the half-empty
glass. "Whiskey." He straightened. "I wonder if it was
doped?"

"Like Penny's?"

Brady knotted his heavy brows. "Yeah. Only her head
was beat in."

Bill shivered, wishing he didn't remember so vividly.

Brady sniffed the glass again, indecisively, and shrugged.
"The doc can tell us." He reached out, touched the grimy
cheek with the back of his hand. "He's getting cold. Dead
at least an hour, maybe more. Nearer two. I hope the doctor gets here quick." Every passing minute would make it
more difficult for the police surgeon to judge the time of
death accurately.

Brady was inspecting the shoddy room, half living
room, half a sketchy dinette with a two-burner plate,
Frigidaire and slatternly cupboards for a kitchen. "Hey!"
He whipped around at Bill. "They won't bring a doc. This
was just a fishing expedition—with a search warrant. We
better meet 'em and send somebody back for the doc." He
was giving the room a quick but thorough scrutiny, flap-
ping his ham-like hand at Bill, "Take a gander around the
bedroom, but hurry."

Bill pushed through the curtain, found another center
fixture and turned on the light. The bedroom, in contrast
to the living room, was lush in a sybaritic, almost feminine
manner. It was obvious where Folsom had his auditions.
Bill checked the oversized Hollywood bed stacked with
satiny pillows, the vanity, draped in more satiny rayon
and studded with crystal jars and bottles that reminded
him of Penny's elaborate array, and a puffed but soiled
slipper chair. In one corner just outside a cretonne-

curtained recess, stood a suitcase that drew his attention. He skipped it and started to push back the cretonne curtain, then realized why the suitcase had caught his eye. It was his! He bent over it, staring at the initials. He straightened, calling, "Jim! Jim Brady! Come here!"

Brady lumbered in, his eyes following Bill's pointing finger. "Hey, I recognize that." He lunged forward, started to pick it up and then drew back. "Fingerprints. Yeah. I know that one. Seen it in your closet." He reached up, swept aside the cretonne curtains. Three suits swung tinkingly on their hangers. "Recognize 'em?"

Bill stared dazedly at the suits. "They're mine. Winter suits I'm not wearing." As Brady dropped the curtain, Bill continued to stared at the alcove. "Do you suppose Gus swiped 'em?"

"That skinny rat couldn't stay in a sleeve of your coat. Naw." Brady grinned tightly. "But I'm beginning to get the picture." In the air he measured a neat rectangle. "And it's got a lovely frame—for you."

Yes, Bill could see that. Then he saw the flaw. "But, Brady, you've been with me. You know I couldn't have done it. You even recognized the suitcase as one I had in the house. You know I couldn't have brought it here."

Brady nodded with grim satisfaction. "I know it. But does the killer know I know it?"

"But this is Folsom's place. You know I never heard of it till this evening."

"And if Folsom says you did? And he lent it to you? Sure, I know the truth, but if anything happens to me . . ." He glanced once more around the room and walked back to peer at Gus through the curtained doorway. "I sure wish we could get the doc up here in a hurry." He nodded toward the window. "You go meet 'em. Send somebody back for the doc. It'd take an extra hour if we waited till they got here."

Bill laughed. "And leave you here where something could happen to my alibi? Nix. We stick together."

Brady grinned. "Real pals, huh?" He took another swift survey of the room, and Gus. "Won't anybody disturb him. The doc's the important thing now." He headed for the door. "Let's go."

Bill swung the MG around and headed down the rutty snake-track road.

This time the rock loomed on Brady's side of the car, and the big man ducked as it loomed over them and whisked past. As Bill straightened out the little car he saw the flash before he heard the splintering crash of the windshield, saw it star in glittering splinters. Brady lurched, straightened with a groan and then toppled across Bill's arms, jerking them off the wheel, pinning them in his lap. He was helpless to guide the speeding car.

He could see the headlights veer off wildly, touching the tops of the scrub pines. Then the pines seemed to wheel over and rush at him. In the hurtling car his body felt weightless yet bound. He saw, with startling clarity in the bright headlights, a single birch among the wheeling pines. He heard the first tinny crunch of metal and the lights went out. . . .

It was the agony in his arm that brought him to. He had to move it and he couldn't. He could feel moist earth against his hand, but his fingers wouldn't even close to scrabble for a hold so that he could shift his arm. It was outside him somewhere, a long way off, but it was still his arm it still hurt. The rest of him didn't hurt. It was almost as if he were the appendage and his arm was his whole being racked with white-hot agony. He opened his mouth in the blackness to scream and scratchy, woolly stuff filled his mouth. The scratchy, woolly stuff pressed against his eyes, too, and flattened his nose so that he couldn't breathe. And something rode heavily on his chest, crushing down against his ribs so that he couldn't even pump for air. Then, suddenly, his arm didn't hurt and he didn't particularly care about breathing. It was just nice and dark in here, dark as the inside of Death. Just let the blackness get deeper and quieter.

It didn't get quieter. He heard, with sharp, ringing clarity, the spang of a stone against the metal of the car, then a little fall of pebbles and the scrape of feet. They've come to save us! He tried harder to breathe, so they wouldn't be disappointed, but the effort was too great and he quit. The feet came to a halt, very close.

"They're both dead."

Under the canopy of the inverted car the words sounded tinny, like something shouted in a bucket.

Bill felt his arm being lifted—the one that was outside him somewhere, not the one curled around Brady in a parody of affection. Fingers moved along his wrist, tightened.

"It's Taylor, all right. I recognize the watch." Pause. "No pulse. He's dead."

Somewhere off another voice spoke but Bill couldn't hear the words. The voice with the feet said, "You got the cop before they went over. In the head."

Murmur: "Okay, okay. But I gotta get his fingers around the butt so it'll look natural."

Feet-Voice was squeezing his fingers around the butt of a gun.

"That oughta tell the story. Brady gets the set-up at the cabin, Taylor makes a break and shoots the cop. Then they crack up." The voice chuckled. "Even a cop can't read that wrong."

Murmur: "I'm coming, but I gotta check. Gun that shot Gus and the cop in his hand. His clothes at the cabin with Gus. That ought to do it." Chuckle. "And when they find it killed Feeney! Sews it up!" Another chuckle. "You sure like to knock 'em off. Let's get some champagne and celebrate." The scrabbling footsteps died and the voice went away.

Bill tried to fight the blackness, to move that arm, open those fingers, to get rid of the gun. He braced his feet against the inverted floorboard and shoved. Hot, black agony welled through his arm, burst through his body and exploded somewhere inside his head.

Just as he was going out he remembered what Brady had said: "If anything happens to me . . ." It had happened. Brady was dead.

Chapter XXI

"You've been dead eighteen hours. That's long enough. After that, you're loafing."

Bill stretched luxuriously and then winced. He felt along his damaged arm. And the top of his head seemed to be made of sore blotting paper. He reached up and felt of it tentatively, mildly surprised to find that it was firm and unyielding. He grinned at Miss Emily. "You mean I can get up?"

"Or you don't eat."

"How's Brady?" He sat up, nursing his sore arm.

Miss Emily snorted in well simulated indignation. "About as well as can be expected from a man who's being nursed by a beautiful colleen. Personally, I've always considered a homely nurse one of the greatest boons to male health."

"You can't recruit nurses for my hospital." He swung his long legs free of the covers and stared at them. He jerked the cover into a voluminous toga. "Hey! Get me some pants!"

A few minutes later Bill, fully dressed, stopped in the adjoining room where Brady, sporting a rakish, lop-sided turban of bandages, was tenderly regarding a diminutive brunette. Brady took his eyes from his wife long enough to pat the bed beside him. "Come on in. This is Mary. Mary, this is the other corpse, Bill Taylor."

Mary shivered in honest distress. "Please, Jim! Don't say things like that. I'm scared enough every time you go out, without that to think about."

"Stuff!" Brady ruffled his wife's black bangs down over her eyes and winked at Bill. "You can't kill an Orangeman by shooting him in the head." He fingered the bandage tenderly. "But you can give him a helluva headache. Did you see who did it, Bill?"

"That waits till after lunch!" Miss Emily bellowed from down the hall. "I'll not let anyone spoil good food with detecting."

She didn't, and it was nearly forty minutes later that the three of them, Miss Emily, Brady and Bill, were back in Brady's room with the newspapers spread around them while Mary was off tending to some wifely duty. Bill smoothed out the newspaper and backed off a little from his black-and-white image staring up at him.

"MILLIONAIRE AND DETECTIVE DIE IN MYSTERY CRASH" was a banner headline, and straggling under it in lesser type: "W. C. TAYLOR DIES IN CRASH FOLLOWING SHOOTING OF DETECTIVE F. M. BRADY. THIRD BODY, TENTATIVELY IDENTIFIED AS TAYLOR'S FATHER-IN-LAW, FOUND IN NEARBY CABIN."

The body of the story went on:

"Mystery still shrouds the deaths yesterday of William Carey Taylor, 32, and his police bodyguard, F. M. Brady, 29, of the District Attorney's staff. The two men were found pinned under Taylor's high-speed racing car in a ditch fourteen miles out of town and less than half a mile from a cabin in which Taylor's father-in-law, Augustus P. Hutzler, said to be a New Jersey real estate man, was found shot to death. Detective Sergeant Brady had been shot through the head and Taylor apparently died from the accident that followed the shooting, according to County Police Chief, Samuel E. Evans, one of the first to reach the scene of the accident. Hutzler's body was found in the nearby cabin during a routine check for witnesses to the shooting and crash, which took place on a lonely section of Hunt Ridge Road. A gun found under the overturned sports car had been recently fired, according to Chief Evans, and is now being checked by State Police Laboratory ballistics experts. Pending outcome of these tests officials are making no statements regarding the shooting and subsequent accident, nor are they tying in the fatal shooting of Taylor's father-in-law to the shooting of the police officer.

"Charles Fentress, of the District Attorney's staff, stated today that in view of the recent death of Mrs. W. C. Taylor, exotic night club singer, and the lack of other heirs, William Carey Taylor will be declared to have died intestate and the Commonwealth will seize the estate for the use of the State Education Fund. . . ."

Bill shoved the paper aside. "Can he do that?"

"He can try," Miss Emily assured him.

"But that thing . . ." He stabbed down at the paper and found Brady had scooped it over on the bed and was reading avidly. "That thing practically says I shot Gus and then killed Brady and wound up killing myself in a ditch."

Miss Emily clucked dolorously. "You can't believe a thing you read in the papers, even my papers."

"But why should Fentress let you get away with this?" He tapped the paper. "Letting us play dead?"

"Maybe he thinks you're better off playing dead than being it."

"Wrap that up. I'll take it." He scowled at the article again. "Hey, this doesn't mention Feeney in connection with that gun."

Miss Emily smirked. "Wouldn't it be odd if somebody else did?"

"A trap?" He thought that over and shook his head. "Why should the killer even come near that particular trap? He's done his job, tied it all up neatly and handed it to the police."

"There's the bait." Miss Emily's finger underscored the closing paragraph. "An awful lot of bait."

Brady started a vigorous nod, thought better of it and said, "Yeah. Forces somebody to come forward and claim the estate. The killer. Because the killer feels safe now."

"A safe man is a dangerous man—to himself."

"Man?"

Miss Emily straightened in her chair and Brady raised himself on one elbow. Bill could feel them staring at him as he tried to figure out why he had questioned the word "man." It came a little slowly through the fog of the accident. "I heard a voice. I remember thinking then that it sounded like someone talking into a bucket. You know, all hollow and distorted. Only it was my head in the bucket. But I couldn't swear it was a man. I think it was, but I couldn't swear to it. But I do know this. There were two people and one of them was a woman. He paused, reasoning it out. "Now why do I know that?" He stared at Miss Emily without seeing her broad, rugged face. Suddenly he grinned. "The champagne!"

"We was not drunk!" Brady held up one hand in solemn oath.

"Not us—them. When a man wants to celebrate something with another man he suggests whiskey or beer, but if he's celebrating something with a woman, something important, it's champagne."

Miss Emily wrapped both hands around her stick and blinked over them at Bill. "I knew there had to be a woman in it." Bill felt himself looking blank and Miss

Emily pounded her stick impatiently. "The phone calls. To Western Union and to me. There had to be an accomplice! And Bill proved there was one—out at the crash. The champagne celebrator." Both the men nodded. "She needn't be important. All that was needed was a voice on the telephone. True, the one to me had to sound like Penny and know some things Penny knew, but to make his plans the killer had to know those things anyway. The call to Bill that Penny took?" Miss Emily hesitated. "Did it have to be a man? Or somebody pretending to be a secretary?" She shrugged. "In any case we've only got Bill's word that there ever was such a call. His one witness is dead. Penny."

"Sorta like your call, Miss Emily? Nobody but you to say you got it," Brady interposed mildly, "since your witness is dead. Same witness. Penny."

"Touché." Miss Emily grinned at him, then faded into thoughtfulness.

"Well, we know Janet couldn't have made the Western Union call," Bill broke the silence. "She was home, sick. And Penny was with her."

"Still the same witness." Brady shook his head at Bill, winced and felt of the bandages. "And still dead."

"It's a pattern. This killer likes dead witnesses." Miss Emily pounded with the knob of her tick. "Dead witnesses! Bill, we've been going at this whole thing backwards. And we'd better get going, fast, if we want to turn it around and protect our most important witness."

"Hey!" Brady sat up in bed. "That guy can't go out. He's supposed to be dead!"

Miss Emily was already hurtling out of the room. "And somebody else really will be—if we don't hurry."

Chapter XXII

Even as Bailey whipped the ancient Packard in to the curb Miss Emily was hurtling out of it. She braked to a halt and glared up at the shabby front of a huge brownstone converted to apartments. Bill, nursing his injured arm, stepped out behind her, feeling ill. This was where Janet lived, a genteelly respectable block of a building, uninspired but comfortable. Could it hold the secret of murder?"

He had waited a moment too long. The door was already closing behind Miss Emily's relentless charge. He sprinted up the steps and followed her through the inner door. His head was just level with the second floor when he saw the apartment door opening and heard a prim, rather querulous voice saying, "Yes? Who is it?"

He took his eyes from the thin, spinsterish figure blocking the narrow opening and glanced across the hall at Janet's door. It may have been a trick of light and shadow, but he thought Janet's door was just closing. That was odd. By rights Janet should be at the office, though he couldn't be sure. He hadn't been there himself this past week. Vaguely he heard voices and realized Miss Emily was using what, for her at least, was her gracious-lady voice.

"Martha Busby, surely you remember me. Emily Cole."

"Emily?" A timid head thrust out the slowly widening crack and craned around. "Emily Cole?" Then a high, well-bred squeal, and the door flew open. "Emily Cole! Dearie me! Well, well. Emily Cole! It's been years since . . . Cole?" The polite, thin voice hesitated. "But weren't you married? It seems to me I remember reading about . . ."

"You were there, Martha. Bridesmaid. You wore yellow tulle and a leghorn hat and, I must say, it wasn't becoming."

"So I did. So I did." She cocked her head on one side and looked up at the hall's dingy light fixture. "Wasn't it? Becoming, I mean? Perhaps I should have worn pink. I think pink always does something for a girl's complexion."

Looking at the thin face and sallow, muddied skin, Bill decided privately that not even pink would have helped, not even back in the distant past when she had been a girl.

Martha Busby frowned at the light fixture and brought her vague gaze down to Miss Emily's face. "Fred. That was his name. Fred Tilworthy. Have you any children, Emily?"

"Martha, you sent my youngest grandson a silver porringer on his first birthday three years ago."

"Did I? My, how time flies. Grandson? You don't look old enough to have grandchildren, Emily."

"If you'd invite us in where there's light, Martha, you'd see just how old I look and, frankly, it doesn't begin to catch up with the way I feel."

Miss Busby sighted Bill around the bulk of Miss Emily. "Oh, a man. Won't you both come in?"

She tittered nervously and did a crab walk backward into her parlor.

"Do take seats, and we'll have tea in a moment. It is tea-time, isn't it? Time slips by so."

Bill rested his good arm along the mantle and fingered the puff-ball fringe, wondering if they would ever get anything from this fluttery, indecisive old maid for whom time had stood still.

Martha Busby cocked her head inquiringly at Miss Emily. "Emily, dear, you've forgotten to introduce your young man." It was gentle reproof.

Miss Emily swiveled to look at him and turned heavily back to Martha. "Miss Busby, this is Mister Taylor. William Carey Taylor. You knew his father, Bradford Taylor."

Miss Busby nodded graciously. "My! So you're Bradford's son. You've grown."

Since Bill was six feet three and weighed over two hundred pounds, this statement in Martha Busby's sweet, vague voice seemed to call for no comment.

Martha smiled at Miss Emily. "Did Bradford have a brother? Ralph? I thought he was rather sweet. He died recently, I think. I seem to remember reading about it. About a week or ten days ago, wasn't it? In an accident?"

"A week ago Wednesday," Miss Emily corroborated hurriedly, leaning forward to push out another question.

"Was it? A truly dreadful thing. So sad. A charming young man." Miss Busby had turned back the clock again. "I remember telling Janet about it . . . ." Her tired sweet voice murmured on.

Bill stood there, his hand closing convulsively on the ball fringe, his stomach cold. Janet had known of Ralph's death! And she had pretended not to have heard of it that shocked evening when he had gotten the news!

Miss Emily, with surprising restraint and even considerable gentleness led her back to the important Thursday, and finally to the direct question: "Martha, do you remember last Thursday? Thursday week, that is."

For all her fluttery vagueness Martha Busby was crystal clear about Thursday. She sat stiffly erect in her chair, primly disapproving of Thursdays in general. "I certainly do. It was the maid's day out." Of that Thursday in particular. "And Bulwer-Lytton was sick."

"Bulwer-Lytton," stated Miss Emily around the cracking edges of her patience, "is dead."

"The cat," she explained, tittering.

"Wasn't Janet sick that day, too?"

Martha Busby sighed. "So she said. But she went to sleep while I was reading 'Tamerlan'."

"I remember. You always read 'Tamerlan' beautifully," said Miss Emily with far more tact that Bill had thought possible.

Miss Busby preened. "I like it. But of course I stopped when Janet went to sleep. Or pretended to. I'm not sure which. This younger generation hasn't the respect for the classics we had as girls. That's when I found out Bulwer-Lytton was having kittens." She tittered.

"Bill knows cats have kittens." Miss Emily was working back into form again and then checked herself to inquire graciously, "How did you find out, then?"

"I came home. To feed Bulwer-Lytton. I always do it at noon. Promptly. And to heat the soup. For Janet. I wouldn't do it for everybody, but I knew her mother."

"You left Janet at noon, is that right? Exactly noon?"

Martha Busby tugged her white shirtwaist into place fussily. "I said noon, Emily. I meant noon. Midday. Twelve o'clock."

"And you left Janet alone?" How long?"

Martha Busby's tiny, wistful face crinkled like pink tissue paper, and her pale lips quivered. "I did think you'd be more understanding, Emily. After all, I was alone in the house and Bulwer-Lytton had . . ."

"Kittens. Yes, yes, Martha. Nobody is criticizing you."

"And anyway, she was asleep, so it couldn't have made any difference."

"What time did you go back?"

"Well, I let the soup scorch, I was so nervous, so I had to make more. And there was Bulwer-Lytton." She caught Miss Emily's eye and quailed. "So it was after two when I finally got back with the soup. Well after two. I know I shouldn't have left the child that long, if she was really sick, but it didn't matter. She'd slept the entire time, she told me. So really I don't see . . ."

"I'm not criticizing you, Martha. You did beautifully. Now you took her the soup, some time after two. And Janet told you she'd been sleeping since you left at noon. Was anybody there? Any other visitor, I mean?"

"Not then. Janet was still asleep. But a few minutes later that creature came in. That blonde hussy who stole Bill Taylor right away from under Janet's nose and many's the time she cried over it. Janet, I mean." Her wild blue eyes opened very wide and she covered her pale lips with one thin hand. "Oh, dear! You're Bill Taylor, aren't you? She was your wife, wasn't she? Oh, dear, I do hope . . . But you're dead, too! I read it in the paper." She lowered her hand and regarded him with frank curiosity, as if entertaining ghosts were a regular and rather interesting phenomenon.

Bill had other things to think about. Martha Busby had blown Janet's alibi for Thursday at one fifteen—the telegram alibi—to bits. And she had added other pieces of information that rounded out a picture. Janet had known about Uncle Ralph's death, and Janet had wept over him, jealous of Penny.

Miss Emily was hitching herself out of the green velour chair, and he noticed irrelevantly that one of the antimacassars clung rakishly to the back of her head. "Thank you, Martha. I appreciate all you've done."

"But you haven't had tea! Dear me. Here, I've been sitting and chatting without once thinking of my guests . . ." She whipped herself out of her chair and pattered off toward a beaded portiere.

"Don't bother, Martha. We've really got to go." Miss Emily thumped and thudded her way toward the door, and Bill joined her, feeling strangely ill and yet numb, as if he were in some kind of vacuum.

Miss Emily was fending off Martha Busby's fragile persistence and easing them out the door. In the hall she dropped her efforts at politeness and sagged against the door frame, her eyes suddenly old and tired. "Bill . . ." It was a husky whisper, tinged with surprised awe. "I was right. Terribly right. No alibi."

She shook herself into the molded form of her armorplate suit and took Bill's arm. "We'll see if Janet is in. I'd rather talk to her first."

Numb, almost unthinking, Bill let her lead him across the hall. He didn't really waken until her stick cracked sharply on Janet's door panels. In mild astonishment he watched the door swing slowly open under the impact. It was almost as if he had known from the start that the door would be only ajar, not fully closed.

The door swung inward, revealing the familiar room and the chair that had been his favorite for those gay, casual, long-ago talks with Janet. Today Kenneth Folsom sat there grinning at them, a gun resting on the arm of the chair, pointing negligently toward the door.

Miss Emily reached in with the knob of her stick and hooked the door toward them, closing it with studied gentleness, as if she were afraid of waking someone. She heaved a long, shuddering sigh as the lock clicked into place.

"I suppose we'll have to go to Charles Fentress now." She nodded toward the closed door and silent apartment. "Folsom is dead. Shot. It was meant to look like suicide."

Chapter XXIII

Bill took Miss Emily's arm and guided her to the small side door and the elevator Brady had said was for the Mayor, relatives and big-shot gamblers. It brought them to Fentress' office by the back way through a small anteroom where Casey stood guard at a fractionally opened door.

The square, stocky figure pivoted, finger on lips. Then, as he saw Bill, his eyes widened in astonishment. He whispered huskily, "You was supposed to stay dead." He thought that over, shrugged and stepped away from the slit through which he had been observing Fentress' office. He jerked his thumb at the crack. "She's in there now."

Bill let Miss Emily brush past him.

He was aware, distantly, that Miss Emily was nodding with grim satisfaction, that she had moved aside and was beckoning him. Stiffly he walked over to the door, propped his good hand against the wall, to still his shudders, and squinted. He could see the almost classic profile of the young investigator, a segment of his desk and the back of a chair where someone else was sitting. He maneuvered around until he could see who it was.

Janet sat with her hands clasped on the desk in a tight double fist, her head slightly bent, her lovely, soft mouth trembling. "I only came down to say good-bye, Charles, not to listen to these fantastic charges. They're absurd. Ridiculous."

"There's nothing ridiculous about the charge of murder." Fentress spread his hands on the desk top and seemed to speak to them rather than to Janet. "Besides, it's my job to listen to charges, however fantastic you may think them." He looked up, peering straight across the room, carefully avoiding Janet. His voice managed to be casual, elaborately casual, like a man carefully shirking a feminine outburst. "And just why did you say Bill Taylor murdered this woman?"

"Because he really loved me."

If was the voice he had expected to hear, low, husky, vibrant, but still it shocked him. He shifted at the door, so that he could see another segment of the room, and there she was, slim, beautiful, arrogantly relaxed in her chair.

Penny!

Penny was alive!

He resisted a wild, crazy impulse to rush to her. He must even have made some unconscious motion, for he found Casey's rock-like arm barring his way.

Penny smiled bewitchingly at Fentress. "That's the best reason I can think of. Even if he did bring that girl to the house and tell me to get out. Just ordered me out." She swept her hand out in a violent gesture that still managed to be graceful. "So I went. I was heartbroken, but I went. He must have realized almost right away what a mistake he'd made, that he really loved me. Perhaps they quarreled. I don't know. I do know Bill had a violent temper. Maybe he struck her and then went berserk. After she was dead—well, he must have tried to make it look like burglars killed her, and tried to pass her off as me. We looked somewhat alike. Superficially, that is."

"She's mad!" Janet pushed herself out of her chair, leaning over Fentress. "She's crazy. Bill never looked at another woman!"

"He looked at you, my dear." Penny's voice was honey-sweet. "Frequently." She shifted her attention to Fentress with a gasp. "You know, I wouldn't be surprised if she has been his accomplice. After the first murder, you know. She's so loyal. And he must have had help. On the other murders, I mean."

"And how do you explain them, Mrs. Taylor?"

Penny shrugged, caught at her stole as it slipped and adjusted it. "I don't. But they were probably necessary—from his point of view. I imagine the poor girl's father must have realized very soon there was something wrong. My pictures were all around the house, and even though this girl and I looked somewhat alike, I'm sure her father must have noticed the difference. He had to be silenced, of course."

"Charles, are you going to let this woman sit there and say . . ."

"I am. Sit down, Janet." Fentress could be firm. "Now, Mrs. Taylor, you also suggested he killed this hoodlum, Feeney. Why?"

"Blackmail. He knew something about the murders. That's obvious, isn't it?"

"It wasn't to us. At first."

Penny smiled and lowered her head, watching him with her deep violet eyes. "But of course you soon found out."

"Well," Fentress began with completely false modesty, "we have ways of learning things. We eventually connected them." He smiled at her. "But it was rather astute of you to see the connection."

Penny flipped a hand airily. "Obvious. He was killed with the same gun as the others. The one you found in Bill's hand—in the wreck."

Fentress nodded solemnly. "Ah, yes. Killed with the same gun. Yes, that linked the murders. But it was very clever of you to spot that, Mrs. Taylor. Very clever. And since you're able to put your finger on the salient point so readily, maybe you'll help us. Why should he shoot Brady? That's baffled us, frankly. Brady was his alibi, or so we thought, for the Feeney killing. Supposedly they were in the basement together."

"But don't you see . . ."

Bill could see her leaning forward in her chair, her whole slim body tense with eagerness to impress.

"You *thought* he was an alibi. Suppose he wasn't? Suppose, if Jim had lived, he'd have told you Bill wasn't in the basement. So he had to die. Then Bill took him off on that mad chase through the hills and shot him. Unfortunately, Bill wrecked his car and was killed. If he hadn't been killed he'd have come back with some story about an ambush or something. Not that I think he'd have gotten away with it, Mister Fentress. You're much too shrewd. But a desperate man will try anything."

"Charles!" Janet slammed her purse on the desk. "Bill isn't here to defend himself. He's dead. But I can't let this creature blacken his name."

Fentress looked up blandly. "Why, Janet, I think she's doing a remarkable job of reconstruction." Penny smiled tightly and he nodded to her. "Especially for a person who was on her way to Mexico when all this happened." He hesitated. "Mrs. Taylor, incidentally, why didn't you return the minute you read of the murder?"

Penny opened her eyes very wide. "But I didn't read of it for days. I was just traveling and trying to put all my sorrow out of mind. In fact, it wasn't until I read of Bill's death that I even felt safe."

"I can imagine."

"So I flew right back."

"There's just one little thing, Mrs. Taylor, that strikes me as odd." Fentress studied his fingertips and smiled at her. "You said the same gun killed Gus, Brady and Feeney. Where did you get that information?"

Penny hesitated. "The papers. It was in the papers."

"I'm afraid it wasn't, Mrs. Taylor. It was very specifically kept out of the papers. At our request."

Penny narrowed her eyes at him speculatively. Her tongue flicked out, as if she'd like to lick back the words she'd spoken.

Fentress watched her for a moment before he raised his voice. "You may bring them in, Casey."

Bill, released from Casey's barring arm, flung open the door and strode into the room. Penny screamed and cowered for a moment in her chair. Janet whirled from the desk, stared at him and went white. One hand went out appealingly. "Bill!" He got to her just in time for her to sag gently against him, and together they faced the woman in the chair.

Penny wasn't done yet. She sat silent a moment, staring at them; then a tight cat-smile teased at her mouth. She nodded to Fentress. "Lovers! She was his accomplice, just as I suspected. I'm sure if you search her apartment you'll find some incriminating evidence. Some very incriminating evidence."

Miss Emily, barging to the center of the room, braked herself with her stick. "We're already found it."

Penny smiled boldly up at Bill. "Then it is going to be awkward, isn't it? Especially since Jim Brady isn't here as an alibi. Poor Jim."

Miss Emily harrumphed with gusto of a water-buffalo. "Yes, poor Jim. You knew him?"

"No. I read it in the papers."

Miss Emily shook her head. "Not in the papers."

For an instant fear flickered in Penny's eyes and then she smiled, waved one hand airily. "Or heard it somewhere."

"Somewhere between here and Mexico?" Miss Emily peered questioningly. "I don't think so. But there's one place you could have heard it." She pivoted majestically. "Bill!"

Bill took his sick eyes off his wife long enough to glance at Miss Emily. "What?"

"When could someone have overhead you calling Brady 'Jim'?"

It still didn't register, not for a moment. Then he got it. "Oh. At the cottage, when we found Gus. Or where Feeney was shot." He hesitated. "Or Folsom knew him as Jim. He might have told her."

Penny nodded abruptly. "Yes, now that I think of it, that's where I heard it."

Miss Emily shrugged massively. "We can ask him."

Penny laughed then. "Go ahead. Ask him."

Again Miss Emily shrugged. "We will. As soon as he comes out of the operating room."

"Operating room?" For the first time panic showed. Penny gathered herself, fussing with her stole, shifting her feet, peering uncertainly about. "Is he ill?"

"He's been shot. I think, when he recovers, he's going to be mad enough to tell the whole story. Everything." Miss Emily made it sound very convincing, even to Bill, who had seen Folsom staring and smiling and silenced forever.

"He's dead!" Penny flung it out defiantly.

"You thought Bill was dead." Miss Emily said it very quietly.

For an instant Bill felt Penny's eyes rake his face with hot, furious hatred. "Ken's dead. He committed suicide!"

"That isn't the way he tells the story," stated Miss Emily with an accuracy that skirted the truth by a wide margin.

"He's dead; I saw . . ." She clapped one hand over her lips and pulled downward, twisting her mouth sidewise, her big, deep eyes suddenly shallow with fright. She leaned on the edge of the desk, pleading with Fentress. "He can't testify against me, can he? A husband can't testify against his wife, can he?"

"Is Bill going to testify against you?"

"Not Bill!" Her eyes whipped him with such scorn and hatred that Bill flinched. "Not him. Ken! He can't testify. A husband can't . . ."

"But Mrs. Taylor, you're just been telling me that Bill is your husband. As I understood it, you expected to inherit his fortune. You told me . . ."

She brushed that aside frantically. "It's Ken. He's my husband. I can prove it. I can show you . . ." She scrabbled in the immense saddlebag of her purse, her hands shaking, her face white under the rouge, making her skin look dirty and splotched. "Ken's my husband, all right. So he can't testify against me."

Fentress sat forward, elbows on the desk, fingers tented. "A husband cannot be *forced* to testify against his wife, or wife against husband."

"That's what I said." Penny spoke wildly, without looking up. "And I'll prove we were married."

Fentress sighed. Bill thought it just a shade dramatic but it was effective. "You have a layman's view of the law, I'm afraid. A husband may, if he wishes, testify against his wife. Except, of course, as to things that occurred in the bedroom."

The sense of what he had said seemed to penetrate slowly. It stilled Penny's clawlike rummaging first. Then her frenzied chatter dribbled off into painful silence. Finally she laughed softly. "He won't testify." She smiled at Fentress. "In fact, I think I like it better with Ken alive." She even twinkled at Miss Emily. "Yes, I like it much better with Ken alive. You'll be surprised at the story he'll tell. Very much surprised."

Miss Emily managed to look crushed which, for a person of her bulk, was no mean achievement. "What story?"

"Why, he'll confirm what I've said—that Bill fell for that stupid little dancer and dared to bring her out to my house! Ken knows about it. She was one of his girls. He knows how I just had to run away, I was so humiliated. And that'll prove just what I've been saying—that Bill killed her." She drew herself up magnificently. "And he'll hang!"

Miss Emily lowered herself into a chair wearily, as if defeated. "Ken Folsom will back up that story?"

"Of course."

"Even now?"

"What do you mean—even now?"

"Now that you won't inherit Bill's money. Now that you won't have five million dollars to pay him off with?"

"Who says I won't?" Once again Penny flicked her eyes so coldly over him that Bill shivered. "Once he's hanged, who says I won't get his money?"

Miss Emily smiled. "Why you did, my dear. If Ken is your husband, surely you can't expect to inherit Bill's money."

That was when Penny fainted.

Chapter XXIV

"She would have gotten away with it, if it hadn't been for Gus. He was just a little too greedy." Miss Emily glared around challengingly and then wriggled herself more firmly into her chair, satisfied that no one intended to refute her.

Bill sat on the leather couch, feeling empty, drained. Not even Janet beside him seemed real at the moment. He would wake up later, but right now he was seeing Penny as they led her away, screaming foulnesses back at him. What a fatuous fool he had been to think she had ever loved him.

He could see the whole story now, as Miss Emily outlined it. Penny had wanted the Taylor millions. There was even a suggestion that she had made an unsuccessful play for Ralph before she switched to Bill. She had a slight handicap, however: Ken Folsom was her husband. But for a promised share of the millions he could be kept quiet. Indeed, knowing now about Folsom, Bill could easily believe he had encouraged the match. Love had never seemed to play a large part in Penny's life, not even with Ken.

Miss Emily had established that when she investigated the death of her son, Freddy. Penny and Folsom had been working the old badger game during the war, selecting service men from wealthy families, usually men with commissions, for whom scandal would mean ruin. Penny had lured them to cheap hotel rooms and Ken "caught" them there, an outraged husband. Most of them paid off. Freddy hadn't.

When Miss Emily told of that, her rugged old face softened. "I knew he wasn't coward enough to kill himself. Or foolish enough to pay blackmail. But he didn't know how dangerous those two were, or how perilous their own positions were. You see, she and Ken weren't married then. It was all a bluff. So if Freddy had gone to the police, those two would have been arrested. They had to stop him, and they made it look like suicide—a sordid little suicide the police could believe in.

"After that they didn't take any more chances. They got married. Legally." Miss Emily nodded grimly to Fentress. "You can check the records. The marriage was *after* Freddy's death.

"Bill looked even better as a husband than as a shakedown. What could they get out of a doting uncle but a few thousand? But as Bill's wife Penny was right next to five million dollars. The only trouble was, Bill didn't give a hoot about it. He didn't even try to get any of Ralph's money. He just wanted to live and earn his own way, so being married to Bill did her no good."

Janet squeezed Bill's arm convulsively and smiled up at him.

Miss Emily went on. "However, there was just one man between her and a fortune—Ralph Taylor. Now I know Ralph. He likes to know all about people, so he started looking into Penny's past. Now he not only stood between her and a fortune, but he was getting dangerous."

For the first time Bill saw the possibility. "They killed Uncle Ralph!" Revulsion choked him.

"A loosened bolt, a leak in the brake line. So easy." Miss Emily's hands knotted convulsively on her stick "He was so vulnerable. But I don't suppose we'll ever know if they killed him. It could have been just a convenient accident—convenient for them. But it set the scene for something we know was murder."

"Why couldn't she leave it at that? Once I inherited Uncle Ralph's money I'd have given her anything she wanted."

Miss Emily shook her head vigorously. "Penny had set herself in a cleft stick. Any day she risked exposure as a bigamist—from any accidental source. And there was always Folsom, as greedy as she, with a propensity for blackmail she knew only too well. By this time she had to eliminate Bill—or Ken. Folsom was on guard. Bill wasn't. But another death, however 'accidental,' that cleared the way for her inheritance certainly would be investigated thoroughly. Police are suspicious of deaths that conveniently clear the way to a fortune, and Penny knew it. But her own 'death'—that was different."

Fentress nodded agreement. "It shifted the picture."

"And it nearly got Bill hanged, which was what she wanted."

"It was an almost perfect set-up." Fentress sounded almost admiring. "It fooled us."

"Too perfect," Miss Emily disagreed. "Once you even suspected Bill wasn't guilty—and I knew he wasn't—it was too perfect. It had to be rigged. Look at it this way. If Bill wasn't lying about that phone call, who could have made it? Somebody imitating Dick well enough to fool Penny? That isn't as easy as it sounds. But suppose Penny simply said it was Dick. Bill was in the shower. He always showered at that time and could be counted on not to answer the phone. Penny simply took a call, probably a pre-arranged one from Folsom, and told Bill it was about the appointment, the Big Opportunity. She knew about it. She'd goaded him into the deal in the first place. So she knew he'd go on that appointment—out to an improbable alibi. It became even more improbable after she destroyed the memo she knew he'd mention."

"We knew of a number of people who knew enough about that deal to have made that call," Fentress pointed out.

"And fool Penny into thinking it was Dick? No. But that alone wasn't enough to point to Penny. Look at the rest. It adds up. That call to me, for instance. The doctor insisted Penny—he meant the corpse mistaken for Penny, we know now—must have been dead or unconscious when that call was made. But it was made. I got it. That call, of course, was meant to hang Bill. But who could imitate Dick to Penny, and Penny to me? Penny, of course. Who would be most likely to intercept the letter notifying Bill of Ralph's death? Penny. And who had access to the office any time she wanted it, to send that telegram? Penny. Except she seemed to have an alibi for that hour. It was just too much Penny. But I couldn't be sure until I broke that alibi. Janet was too groggy with sleep to do anything but accept Penny's statement that it was one o'clock. However, Martha Busby remembered the time, thanks to Bulwer-Lytton."

"Bulwer-Lytton?" Fentress blinked in astonishment and then laughed as Miss Emily explained.

"From then on Penny was in the clear," Miss Emily continued. "Who looks for alibis for a dead person?"

"But who was the girl who was killed?" Bill still held the memory of that awful moment when he had opened the kitchen door. "I took her for Penny."

"You were meant to. Folsom had access to hundreds of girls. Easy enough for him to pick out one who resembled Penny and bring her to the house."

"And they killed her? Just for money?"

"Not 'they'—Penny. Folsom hurried down to The Rendezvous for a rehearsal, to clear himself. That was important, too. Penny couldn't afford to have the least suspicion pointed at him. You, Bill, were to have that honor. That's why they doped the girl first, with that Scotch highball. The Scotch was a mistake and you noticed it, Bill. A little thing but it kept nagging me. They doped her so Penny could handle her later, when she was sure Folsom's alibi was established, and yours wasn't. They probably got her up there on pretense of rehearsal for some show. And more than likely went through with one. That would account for the girl's fingerprints all over a suspiciously clean house."

Fentress leaned forward. "And how was all this to have worked, Miss Emily? Admitting the police were fooled—and for a time we were."

"Oh, it was to be simple. Bill's phony alibi was to have convicted him, plus Penny's carefully planted 'bruises.' You'll notice she picked a man to 'see' them—a woman would have spotted them as daubs of makeup immediately. Only she didn't figure on Cameron putting them forward through somebody else, and making us suspicious." Miss Emily spread her big hands over her stick. "On that evidence the police should have convicted Bill and, in due time, hanged him. With Bill dead, Penny would have returned from 'Mexico' with the same story she told, a woman driven from her home, Bill's rages, the new girl-friend murdered. As a gently weeping widow she could have put it over, too. And in time she'd have collected five million dollars. Later, I suppose, she would have 'married' Folsom. But Gus came along."

"Yes, Gus came along." Fentress studied the far corner of the room. "They planned everything else so carefully it's a wonder they didn't pick an orphan for a victim."

Miss Emily flapped one hand. "I imagine they thought they had. On Maggie's application she probably listed herself as an orphan. No one in her right mind would claim Gus if she didn't have to."

Bill tucked Janet's arm under his and leaned forward. "Just how did Gus upset things?"

"You saw him. He was greedy. And we know those pictures of Penny made him suspicious. He took that picture around to The Rendezvous and on to Folsom's, asking questions. I think he got too many answers and Penny had to eliminate him. It must have been Penny. Folsom, we know, stayed at the office. Bill and Brady saw him there."

"And Feeney?"

"Gus' questions at The Rendezvous may have given him ideas, or he may even have seen Penny alive! We do know what he planned to do. A little blackmail. So he knew something, or thought he did. Penny either followed him or just happened to be slipping in the back door to check Folsom's office and see that anything incriminating had been cleared out. She didn't trust Folsom too much. Look what happened to him, when he was no longer useful, perhaps even dangerous."

"Can we pin that one on her?"

"She knew he was dead even before you did, Charles. A little police work ought to do the rest. I suspect his death, even though it was meant to look like suicide, was intended to incriminate Janet, or at least give her a very uncomfortable time. Like Janet's letter she swiped and planted. You see, Penny may not have loved Bill, but she was feminine enough to want to do Janet in. She knew they were in love."

Bill glanced down at Janet and grinned. For that much perception, at least, he had to give Penny credit. His arm tightened around Janet's shoulder and she leaned against him with a warm, pleasant casualness that was more exciting than any amount of demonstrativeness.

"Well, that's that, Charles." Miss Emily heaved herself to her feet and beamed at him. "I'm glad I could help you."

"Oh, you've done remarkably, Miss Emily. I have

to thank you particularly for smoking out Penny with those newspaper articles. We were wondering just how to do it."

Miss Emily jerked back in the midst of one of her ponderous pivots. "What! You knew it wasn't Penny who was murdered?"

Fentress grinned easily though his eyes slid away from Janet. "Oh, yes. Almost from the start."

"But—but—" Miss Emily seemed dazed. "How?"

"Routine," croaked a voice behind Bill, and Casey came past him to the desk. He laid an official paper down meticulously.

"Casey's right. Routine. When the fingerprint check was made, we knew the dead girl had been working in a war plant in New Jersey in August of 1945. But the only reliable date we had for Penny was V-J Day—August, 1945—when we know she was in Pasadena. The conflicting stories we heard about 'Penny' then made sense. There were two girls and the dead one *wasn't* Penny Wise."

"And you didn't tell Bill his wife wasn't dead?"

Fentress looked unhappy. "No, because we weren't sure he wasn't involved. It could have been any of a number of things, including an insurance swindle. Men have connived with their wives on tricks like that before. It wasn't until last night we were sure he was clear. From then on things moved a little fast."

For a moment Miss Emily scowled ferociously and then whooped with laughter. "Charles, you may make a decent district attorney yet. Count on the support of my papers when the time comes."

Fentress accepted this with a grave nod, and there was just a touch of smugness in the parting glance he gave Janet as Bill led her out into the corridor. Bill squeezed Janet's arm and they turned back to wait for Miss Emily, holding hands companionably.

Bill heard Miss Emily's stick tap the desk and her voice boomed out. "What's that? Warrant for Penny's arrest?"

"This?" Paper crackled sharply; then Fentress coughed. "It's the permit for burial. It's made out in Penny's name, but . . ."

Miss Emily grunted fiercely. "Leave it like that. She'll be late for her funeral. But not too late, I hope."

The Authors

Douglas Stapleton was born Samuel Granville Staples (1907-1972) and grew up in Virginia. Douglas Stapleton may have started out as a pen-name, but appears to have been taken on for most professional use. According to one newspaper article, Stapleton "started out as a song-and-dance man with Eleanor Powell in her first success, 'The Wedding of the Painted Doll,' became historical correlator for the *Encyclopedia Britannica*, advertising man with General Foods, program manager for a radio station and radio commentator and (in Washington) administrator for the W.P.A. and later Radio Expert for the executive office of the president." After service in the naval reserve and teaching at the Ft. Monmouth signal corps O.C.S., he worked as an advertising executive in New York for a wide variety of TV and radio programs. As an author, Stapleton wrote a multitude of books, articles, short stories, radio plays, and television comedies.

It was while working in New York that he met and married his third (?) wife, Dorothy, in 1941. Dorothy Tucker Aden (1917-1970) was from Bastrop, Louisiana, where she had worked as a political speechwriter, theatrical company press agent, licensed engineer, radio station operator, film director and producer, and creator and writer for the army radio serial, 'This is Your Judge Advocate.'

Douglas and Dorothy Stapleton

She moved to New York to become director of radio, TV and films for Grey Advertising, where she met Douglas. While on their honeymoon, they co-produced a Broadway play, 'Questionable Ladies,' and wrote their first novel together, *The Corpse is Indignant*. For that mystery Dorothy used the pen-name Helen A. Carey. In future collaborations, the pair went by Douglas and Dorothy Stapleton. They continued to work together on radio shows, monthly magazine columns, and other projects. *American Magazine* called them "the people who work 48 hours a day." (For relaxation, they both obtained their pilot's licenses.) They 'retired' to Virginia Beach in 1951, becoming involved in community work and some further mystery writing for Arcadia House (*Late for the Funeral, Corpse and Robbers*, and *The Crime, the Place, and the Girl*). This retirement didn't last long, as they had moved to Monroe, Louisiana, in 1953 to help operate a new radio station, though it shut down the next year. Their mystery novel writing ended after the mid-1950s (though short stories for mystery and science fiction magazines were published into the 1960s), and they appear to have lived their final years in Los Angeles, California.

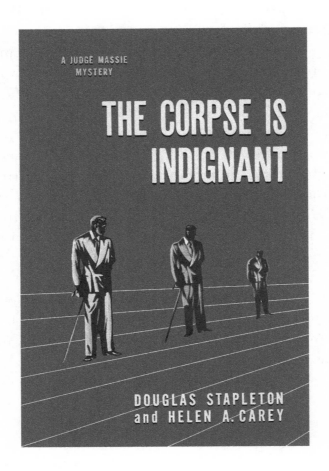

A JUDGE MASSIE
MYSTERY

THE CORPSE IS
INDIGNANT

DOUGLAS STAPLETON
and HELEN A. CAREY

Details at
CoachwhipBooks.com

Available from your favorite online retailers

DEAD
WEIGHT
ADDISON
SIMMONS

Details at
CoachwhipBooks.com

Available from your favorite online retailers

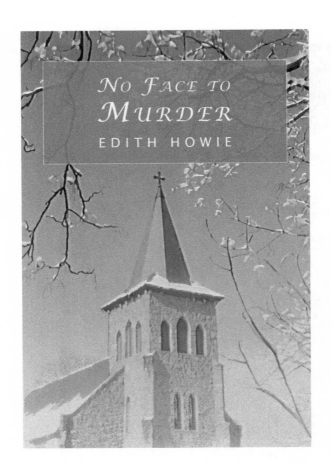

Details at
CoachwhipBooks.com

Available from your favorite online retailers

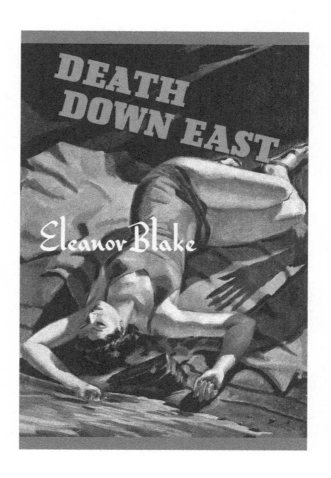

Details at
CoachwhipBooks.com

Available from your favorite online retailers

THE
RUMBLE
MURDERS

Henry Ware Eliot, Jr.

Details at
CoachwhipBooks.com

Available from your favorite online retailers

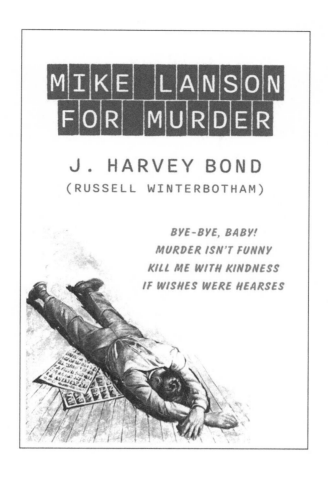

MIKE LANSON
FOR MURDER

J. HARVEY BOND

(RUSSELL WINTERBOTHAM)

BYE-BYE, BABY!
MURDER ISN'T FUNNY
KILL ME WITH KINDNESS
IF WISHES WERE HEARSES

Details at
CoachwhipBooks.com

Available from your favorite online retailers